THE ULVERSCROFT...

A new Chi...
at Moor...

Twin op...
Western Op... London.

The Frederick... Chair of
Ophthalmology at the University of Leicester.

Eye Laser equipment to various eye hospitals.

If you would like to help further the work of the
Foundation by making a donation or leaving a
legacy, every contribution, no matter how small, is
received with gratitude. Please write for details to:

THE ULVERSCROFT FOUNDATION,
The Green, Bradgate Road, Anstey,
Leicester LE7 7FU, England.
Telephone: (0533) 364325

MANHATTAN MAGIC

A lonely newcomer to the New York stockbroking firm, Ellen was disconcerted to be advised by the first personable man she met to return to the safety of England. Don Redman implied she was too young, too green to make out in this cut-throat world. It was a challenge Ellen was determined to meet.

JEAN DAVIDSON

◆

MANHATTAN MAGIC

Complete and Unabridged

LINFORD
Leicester

First published in Great Britain in 1988 by
IPC Magazines Limited
London

First Linford Edition
published December 1990

British Library CIP Data

Davidson, Jean
    Manhattan magic. — Large print ed. —
    Linford romance library
    I. Title
    813.54[F]

    ISBN 0–7089–6928–3

Published by
F. A. Thorpe (Publishing) Ltd.
Anstey, Leicestershire
Set by Words & Graphics Ltd.
Anstey, Leicestershire
Printed and bound in Great Britain by
T. J. Press (Padstow) Ltd., Padstow, Cornwall

1

NEW YORK CITY! It was laid out before her, the red taillights of cars streaming slowly along the straight streets. Lights blazing from apartment towers, and from office blocks — enthusiastic employees working late, she imagined, in their striving for the top. If she opened the window — impossible because of the reinforced double glazing — she would let in the pulsating throb of the town, perpetually awake, perpetually busy. From her twentieth-floor vantage point she could see, if she craned her neck, the famous outline of the Empire State Building, and there, to the north, was the dark patch of Central Park.

Ellen sighed and leaned to switch on a lamp before drawing the curtains to shut out the sight. As she did so, the unmistakable wail of a police car siren was funnelled up to her. She found it a very lonely, eerie sound.

New York: The most exciting city in the world and she, Ellen J. Huntsworth, not yet twenty-four years old, an Englishwoman, was privileged to work here. She should be ecstatic, overjoyed, thrilled at the opportunity. And she had been, when she arrived; eager to get started on her new life, excitedly waiting for her first real view of the town as the taxi bore her from the airport.

But she wasn't any longer. It had all worn off, like gilt from a cheap watch. Only two weeks here, and she was desperately homesick. She missed the gentle hazy sunshine of a London morning, the green open spaces, her friends. She even missed her family, something she never expected to feel.

Here she was, sitting in this beautiful modern apartment with its smoked glass and chrome tables, ultra modern kitchen, fully tiled bathroom, with nowhere to go and no one to talk to. Ellen hated feeling sorry for herself, but she had to admit that's exactly how she felt.

She'd tried. Very hard. But her please and thank yous in a quiet English voice seemed to make the New Yorkers even more impatient. And at work, the job for which she'd poured out all her energy, heart and soul, she was treated like a shadow. She couldn't understand it — it had never happened to her before. Perhaps she'd never been at the centre of parties, or at work, but she'd always had plenty of friends and entertainment. Yet her American colleagues stared right through her as if she didn't exist.

She moved restlessly about the room, touching the soft leather of the sofa, the polished wood of the bookshelf, as yet bearing only a handful of paperbacks. This time of night was the worst. It was just dark outside and she felt imprisoned. She'd heard so many horror stories about the dangerous streets of New York that she was afraid to go out in the evening.

She caught sight of herself in the large

wall mirror and grimaced. Soft auburn hair, slicked back and falling to her shoulders, large soft brown eyes. "Grrr," she growled at herself, exasperated by the softness, the yearning she saw there. This was no good. This city was here, now, hers for the taking. It would do no good skulking in her apartment, marooned from life. She had to do something. Hadn't her first boss always told her, during her initial stockmarket training, that risk was all? Nothing ventured, nothing gained?

Quickly she picked up her black leather jacket and handbag from where she had tossed them on the breakfast bar as she came in, and went to the door. There were two locks, a bolt, and a safety chain. It was like escaping from Fort Knox, she thought, as she wrestled with them and finally freed herself to step out into the corridor.

She had to admit that the agency had found her a pretty good, if small, place to live, but finding somewhere to live in Manhattan these days was very difficult.

The rent was the absolute top she could afford, but it was very comfortable, secure, and well decorated. There was even a maid service. She walked along the carpeted hall to the lift and punched the button. As usual the lift was empty, and she felt dislocated again, as if she was living on a different time schedule from everyone else.

The marble lobby had a small fountain and fishpond, surrounded with greenery, and felt cool. Just as she was about to go out of the glass doors the commissionaire called out to her, "'Night, Miss Huntsworth," and she turned to answer him. But as she did so the door in front of her resisted her pressure, and she walked right into it. Swinging angrily around she saw a tall, dark man doing just the same on the other side, wanting to come in. He had been talking over his shoulder to someone in a large, shiny, maroon limousine.

They glared at one another through the glass, and in the split second as Ellen was thinking to herself, 'One of us has to give way — and I expect he'll think it will be me,' he gave an ungracious smile and jerked the door open for her.

"Sorry," he said. "I guess I wasn't looking where I was going. Are you all right?"

Ellen stared up in astonishment into clear, grey forthright eyes. "Yes, I'm OK — and I wasn't looking either."

She continued to gaze, and suddenly he smiled. She realised that he was incredibly good looking, tall and well built, dressed in an impeccable charcoal grey suit, and he managed to convey a sense of coiled energy rather than of a tired businessman coming home from work.

"You're not concussed, are you?" he asked. "Only you're staring at me as if I've sprouted horns."

"But — you're English aren't you? And it's the first time anyone's apologised to me since I arrived in New York."

"Half and half — I expect it was the English half who apologised. I can't shake the habit. New Yorkers can be brusque at times. You'll have to learn to push and shove with the rest of them — earn their respect. You sound as if you haven't been here long."

"Just two weeks."

He nodded. "And you're feeling homesick. That'll pass."

His hand was still on the door, but he made no move to go in yet. "What you need is to talk to your friends, then you'll feel better."

"Unfortunately I don't know anyone here — yet," Ellen said as lightly as she could, determined not to betray any of her earlier self-pity, "so I was just going out for a walk."

He frowned, let go of the door, and took a step closer. "What — out there? Are you sure its wise? You can't be in need of fresh air, it's cooler inside."

Ellen, having screwed up her courage, didn't want to be deflected and took a step backwards. "I'm looking forward to it — all life is going on out there."

"Yes — both pleasant and unpleasant."

He shook his head, and as he did so she noticed that in his thick, black hair there were unusual, distinctive flecks of grey. "That's crazy. Why don't you take a cab and see a show?"

"No thanks," Ellen said, determined not to listen to the voice of reason. "I know what I'm doing. You can't get the feel of a place from inside a car."

"Listen, the streets are no place for a young girl. You should wait till you have someone to go with you." And he laid a hand on her arm.

Irritated now, Ellen drew herself up to her full height — at five feet and a few inches making little impression on his height — and said with some asperity, "Less of the young girl, thanks. I've been looking after myself for years."

They glared at one another again, then he said, "Well, please don't go down any dark alleys — stick to the kerbside. Will you promise me that?" And when she gave a reluctant nod, he went in, although his broad back radiated disapproval.

Ellen took a few steps across the pavement, then glanced back. He was exchanging a greeting with Joe, the commissionaire. When he had disappeared into the lift, Ellen went back inside.

"Joe — who is that man?" she demanded. He chuckled. "Got to you, did he? Same effect on all the women. Ah, if only some of it would rub off on me. He's Mr. Redman, Don Redman, twenny-first. Lived here about two years."

"Thanks," she said, before going out again. Don Redman. How had she managed to live in this building for a whole fortnight and not see him? Someone as attractive as that — it wasn't exactly a classically handsome face, but as he spoke and moved he seemed so alive, like a powerful force that would draw others to him. And he lived only on the floor above her. But, handsome or not, he seemed to have one annoying habit — he liked to spread his unwanted advice around, and that was something she hated above all else. She'd fought

9

hard to escape the interference of others in her life, and the last thing she wanted was some stranger starting all over again — assuming they had the misfortune to bump into each other again. She'd been foolish to let slip she was virtually alone in New York. He might be only half British, but he might still feel obliged to seek her out. Ellen gritted her teeth. She'd had enough of feeling self-pity. She certainly didn't want anyone else's pity — that would be unendurable. If they ever met again, it had to be as equals.

On the dot of eight a.m. Ellen entered Geiger Associates, and saw that as usual she wasn't first. She liked to get up early, so had easily slipped into the early habits of the office. By New York standards it was a small firm but old and prestigious, working on two floors of a multi-storey building. The legal division and the senior executives were on the thirteenth, stockbrokers, research and administration on the fourteenth floor. Ellen worked with the other stockbrokers in one vast, open-plan room. The soft carpet was mushroom-coloured, the air conditioning and humidifiers maintained a constant, fresh atmosphere, and there was plenty of airy space and green plants behind the desk. This early in the morning there was an air of expectant calm.

As she walked to her desk she passed blond-haired Mark reading a newspaper, who swivelled his eyes briefly in her direction, his habitual greeting, and Maggie, who gave her a crisp good morning. Maggie was always beautifully dressed in grey or cream linen suits and contrasting blouses which looked as if they came straight from the cleaners each day. Her dark curly hair was cut short, her make-up expertly applied.

Ellen expected that Maggie had noticed she had worn her two best outfits the others had suddenly seemed shabby and outdated — in rotation for two weeks solid. She was waiting impatiently for her first paycheck so that she could rush out to Fifth Avenue and buy some new clothes.

And there was her very own working area. There was her three-way phone, the two video screens where she watched the figures coming through. Through these she kept in touch with current prices, with Wall Street, the City in London, and financial centres throughout the world, depending on the time of day. When she looked up she could see at a glance from the clocks on the wall the time in London, Melbourne, Hong Kong or Tokyo, among others. Also on her desk were a neat pile of files, notebook and clipboard for making notes, and a complex calculator.

For a moment Ellen felt again the heady upsurge of elation at the sight of it all. She had made it! Against all the odds she had succeeded: Albeit only the first step on the ladder, but she was on her way, she knew it, and knew too that she was tremendously lucky to be doing what she wanted, where she wanted.

Two hours later the atmosphere was at its normal electric level. Maggie, Mark, Clyde and all the others were each deeply involved — buying, selling, advising, their voices switching from a low hum to excited shouting. Phones rang, nails clicked on computer buttons. Ellen was pleased that she had managed to satisfy one of her more demanding clients, a Mrs. Goldberg, who telephoned every morning, insisting on knowing her financial position.

For a second she rubbed her neck and shoulder muscles to relax, then became aware of a slight stir in the office. Mr. Abrams, vice-president, was striding towards her.

"'Morning, Huntsworth," he said, tossing a brown file of papers on her desk. He called them all by their surnames, an affectation Ellen was not yet accustomed to. He pulled up a chair and sat down, and she felt a little angry. He hadn't asked if she were free to be interrupted, but then she supposed that as youngest and newest she hadn't earned that privilege yet.

13

"I have a client list here," he was saying. "Five people, all interested in the same portfolio. I want you to run through and come back to me this afternoon with your recommendations. Think you can handle that?"

Ellen pressed her lips together to hide her growing anger. Today had already been hectic, and promised to continue so. If she took this extra work on she would neglect her own clients. But she had not yet had time to sum up Mr. Abrams.

Heart hammering furiously, she said as coolly as she could, "Yes, I can handle that, Mr. Abrams. I will be able to do it for you after work."

He stared at her through black-rimmed glasses. "I said, I need it by this afternoon. The top client will be ringing me back then. You can see," he flipped open the file and pointed to a figure, "that he has plenty to invest."

"I can see that this important list of clients deserves careful attention," Ellen said, determined not to give in.

"I shall devote a lot of time to it this evening — and I expect the clients will appreciate that." Inside she was not as calm as she sounded. She was both angry that he considered she could just drop her own work for him, and also afraid that by standing up to him she would be thrown out on her ear — yet she had to fight.

"Very well, if that's your attitude. But I'll expect it on my desk first thing, and it had better be good," he said heavily before getting up.

Ellen breathed out a long sigh. So, it seemed she had won that skirmish. But by sticking up for herself she might have gained an important enemy. Before she resumed her work she thought she saw Maggie quickly looking away.

By mid-day Ellen was famished, as always. Although she wished her figure was more fashionably slender, she was not overweight and had a healthy appetite. She had dieted once or twice, but it only made her curves more pronounced. She picked up her handbag and stood up.

"Fancy a sandwich at my favourite deli?" Maggie stood by Ellen's desk, also ready to go out.

"Sure, that would be great."

As they made their way down in the lift, Ellen wondered why Maggie had issued her sudden invitation. Perhaps she would learn why she had been nearly frozen out by her colleagues.

When they were seated on high stools, plates of salad and sandwiches on the counter in front of them, Maggie surprised her by saying, "Hey, you know you were great with old Abrams this morning? You handled him real well." And she flashed a smile that lit up her small-featured face, normally wearing an almost fierce expression, like a burst of sunshine.

"Thanks. Although I'm not sure I did the right thing. He was furious."

"He'll forget it. He's tried it out on all of us. In fact, he had me running round in circles for a week till Clyde wised me up."

"That's a relief. I didn't want to be

chucked out as soon as I got here, not after all the struggle it's taken."

"You too?" Maggie managed to eat deftly and neatly yet talked rapidly at the same time. "Everybody thought I was crazy to go into the financial world. Dire warnings about how it would chew me up and spit me out in no time. No place for a woman, they said back in my home town."

"Exactly — even though there are quite a few women in the English Stock Exchange now. It was my parents who resisted the idea most. Some of my friends thought I was a bit weird, getting mixed up in high finance, but Mum and Dad!" Ellen shook her head.

"Did they try to stop you?" Maggie asked with interest.

"I had to finance myself through training at first, till Dad saw whatever he did wouldn't make any difference, then he helped out."

"You're one determined woman. My fights have largely been to get people to take my career seriously. You know, you

17

get introduced to some gorgeous hunk, and when you tell him your job he just laughs as if you're joking."

"I haven't had much time for gorgeous hunks," Ellen admitted, a vision of Don Redman flitting unasked through her mind. "A few boy friends, but nothing . . . I don't know how to explain."

"No one for whom you would gladly give up your career even," Maggie supplied.

"No — never!"

"I guess you must still be finding your feet. What do you think of our little town?"

Ellen thought hard for a moment. "Frightening — at first," she confessed, "but I'm beginning to get used to it, and it's very thrilling to be here."

"Listen, any time you want to eat pasta, I know the best trattoria in town; you just call me — in fact, why not tonight? You'll want a break when you've finished Abrams' work."

"I'd love that."

"Good. By the way," Maggie said,

pushing her empty plate to one side and pulling out a folded newspaper from her bag, "did you see this little piece?"

Ellen took the financial paper and saw that a news item at the bottom of a column had been ringed in ink. *"Rumour has it that Geiger Associates, so long an independant if idiosyncratic force, may not be in a position to resist the advances of one of Wall Street's more hungry sharks."* Ellen read. "What does this mean, Maggie?"

"It means someone wants to buy us — and we may not be strong enough to stop them, which is certainly news to me, and if that happens, who knows what might happen to us?"

Ellen frowned in dismay. To come all this way only to lose out because of a takeover — that was something she couldn't bear to contemplate.

A few days later Ellen woke somewhat bleary-eyed, having been up late the night before at a financial meeting. She stumbled into the bathroom and turned on the shower, to be rewarded shockingly with needles of icy cold water. No amount of fiddling could raise the temperature, so she retreated grumpily to the bedroom to dress, her skin glowing. This made her feel warmer and stickier than a tepid shower would have. She put on her thinnest white cotton shirt with an open collar, grey pinstripe suit, applied her make-up and went to the kitchen to make a reviving cup of coffee. Unfortunately, she found she'd left the milk out of the fridge and it had turned. Disconsolately she opened the fridge and peered inside. One small egg, and some white bread in the freezer. Her stomach growled at her: not enough. She'd been able to nibble only a sandwich at the buffet last night.

At least it was still quite early. Only seven-thirty, the early morning sun a clotted yellow through the city's fumes. Ellen decided to eat breakfast out. She remembered there was an appetising-looking coffee shop just next door,

Arnaldi's Deli, and decided to give it a try.

Joe was in his usual place as she crossed the cool lobby.

"You're early this morning, Miss Huntsworth," he said. "Did the heat wake ya? Going to be a scorcher, they say."

"Too true. And I've run out of food. I'm going to Arnaldi's. Any good?"

"Yeah," he nodded enthusiastically. "They do a great toasted bagel."

"Oh . . . good." Ellen thought she knew what he meant, a bread roll with a hole in the middle.

The city was very much alive when she stepped out. Traffic moved in impatient fits and starts, horns trying to clear the way. Music blared from a ghetto blaster on the building site opposite, and there wasn't a breath of a breeze.

Inside Arnaldi's Ellen looked round in dismay. It looked as if every seat was filled, both the bar stools and the long marble counter and the window, and the tables along the side wall. Steam

21

gushed up from the Espresso machine, sending a wonderful aroma of coffee in her direction. She decided to wait by the sign that said "Please wait to be seated" and gazed coolly into the distance, trying to ignore the gazes from the mostly male customers.

A flustered waitress approached. "How many?" she asked, as if someone might be hiding behind Ellen.

"Just one, please — " she began diffidently.

"This way," the waitress sped ahead of her to a table for two tucked away at the back of the room, and cleared away used plates and cups with quick movements of her hands. Ellen thanked her retreating back and sat down, glancing at the front of the journal held up by her breakfast partner, obscuring his face. *'New England Real Estate'* it read, above a picture of trees in startling autumn colours bordering a peaceful lake. Ellen sighed and picked up the menu. As she studied it she was aware of a quick scrutiny from opposite, but when she glanced up, he — she could tell from the muscular hands, with a few dark hairs on the back — was already hidden. At least she wouldn't be bothered by him.

"Yes?" The waitress was back.

"I'd like — an Arnaldi Special. With coffee, please."

"How you want your eggs?"

Ellen stared blankly. "Oh, er — fried, please."

"Yeah, very funny." The waitress shifted her stance and chewed her gum more aggressively. "I said, how you want your eggs."

"She'd like them over easy," said her companion, laying aside the journal and revealing himself as Don Redman, "and bring plenty of cream with the coffee."

"OK, OK," said the waitress, breaking into a flirtatious grin for him. "Coffee coming right up."

"I suppose I should thank you," Ellen said to Don Redman, trying not to sound grudging. "It's my first breakfast out."

"That Special'll keep you going all

day, that's for sure."

Ellen met his eyes then quickly looked away again. He was, on second meeting, even more improbably attractive than she remembered. His jacket was over the back of his seat, his shirt open at the neck so that she could see the smooth, tanned skin of his neck and he was clean shaven. He was leaning back relaxedly in his chair. Although she had thought about him every day since their first encounter, now they were actually face to face her mind had seized up.

"They say it's going to be a scorcher today," she said at last, thinking, 'Oh dear, can't I be less British than that, talking about the weather?'

"Is that a fact?" Don replied idly, then leaned forward and said, "Miss Ellen J. Huntsworth — tell me, what does the J stand for?"

Ellen blushed scarlet. "It doesn't stand for anything," she admitted. "I'm plain Ellen, although my mother's name is Jennifer. I thought it sounded good."

He laughed, revealing even, white

teeth. "So it does. People would be impressed. But I've got the advantage on you. My name is — "

"Don Redman. How do you do?" Ellen held out her hand, eyes twinkling.

Don raised his brows, then gave a slight nod, and took her hand. "Glad to know you. The score is even. I won't ask you by what devious means you discovered my name."

"I didn't have to bribe Joe," she replied, her smile broader.

"Meaning I did?" He shook his head. "Easier than that — I checked the post boxes for a new name! Still, it looks like you're right, you can take care of yourself, both the other night and now — you've found the best place in town to eat breakfast. So how are you enjoying New York?"

"It's a dream come true to be here," she answered honestly. "I'm loving every minute — or nearly so. I couldn't get any warm water this morning."

He nodded. "A local hazard." Then the smile left his face. "But remember, a lot of people come here with a suitcase full of dreams and, if they're not careful, they either get trampled on or severely disillusioned."

Ellen gritted her teeth, but maintained her pleasant smile. Why did he assume that she was still wet behind the ears, just because she'd remarked that New Yorkers weren't all ultra polite?

"I can take it," she informed him. "I don't intend to go under."

"Good," he said, but he looked as if he didn't really believe her. "But if you ever do need help, you can always come to me."

"I thanked you for rescuing me this morning. I don't intend to summon up any more white knights," Ellen informed him crisply.

"Believe me, there's nothing more important than getting your eggs right," he said lightly, but she detected a steely glint in his deep grey eyes. He wasn't going to give up. "You're not in the least vulnerable then?"

"I've never thought of myself as weak,

no. I've always looked after myself."

"You're telling me you don't need anyone, is that it?" Don was looking at her curiously, and Ellen was unable to meet his eyes. She took refuge in her coffee cup. How could she explain to a virtual stranger why it was important to her to prove she could survive and prosper alone?

The tense moment was broken when the waitress slid two plates in front of her. "One Special," she intoned, then whisked away. Ellen stared at three eggs, the yolks nicely whitened on top, two large slices of gammon ham, a mound of fried potatoes, grilled tomatoes, several slices of toast and, on a separate plate, two bagels. Avoiding Don's eye she picked up her knife and fork, then hesitated, unsure where to start.

"Hope that's the way you like your eggs," he said. "It's the way. I like 'em — can't stand the sight of those yellow eyes staring up at me so early in the morning."

27

"Yes, that's great, it's just I — " She looked up, caught his eye, and they both laughed. "All right, I may not be able to eat it all — but I'm going to try!"

"That's the spirit." And Don leaned back in his chair and calmly watched her.

"Don't let me keep you — from your job. You do work, don't you?" she said, feeling uncomfortable under his gaze.

"Oh yes. But there's time yet." He looked at his watch. "I think I'll have some more coffee," and he signalled to the waitress. "What about you? What job are you dressed so smartly for?"

"I'm a stockbroker. I work for Geigers, it's a good outfit," she replied proudly, lifting her chin and meeting his eyes, defying him to say something derogatory. The clean lines of his face registered surprise.

"Don't get me wrong," he said, "but aren't you kinda young to be running around the world of high finance?"

"I don't see what that's got to do with it. I'm as quick as the next woman — or man. And I'm no beginner. I passed my exams, and I've served my apprenticeship in London."

She hoped she saw a glimmer of respect in his eyes. At least, something flickered there. "You're smartly dressed," he agreed, "but are you smart enough to know what you're letting yourself in for? I've seen plenty of cases of burn out before thirty. You have to live, eat, breathe figures — and one mistake means your reputation sinks to rock bottom, and you have to start all over."

"Please don't lecture me — it's unfair on top of watching me eat three fried eggs — what was it, easy over?"

"Over easy."

"OK. I know what's involved. I've just told you about my training."

Don leaned his forearms on the table, his electric gaze demanding her attention. "No jokes now. Listen to me. What's a nice kid like you doing so far away from home, all on your own, no friends, in just about the world's toughest city, and just about the world's toughest job."

"Well, listen to me!" Ellen returned, annoyed at feeling upset that he'd called her a kid. "I've spent the last six years listening to people telling me what and what not to do with my life. I didn't listen then, and I won't listen now. I love my work, it's what I've always wanted to do — and as for living and breathing it — I dream it too!"

"Maybe so, but there are other things in life besides ambition."

"For a woman, you mean. I don't happen to want those. At least, not now. Is that what upsets you, because I'm a woman in a male preserve?"

Don shook his head and made an exasperated sound. "Don't put words into my mouth that weren't there. Think of this. Do you have what it takes to succeed where so many have failed? And all alone?"

Ellen fiercely buttered a bagel. "Of course I do. Why else would I be here? Now, if you don't mind, I want to finish my breakfast."

But Don wasn't finished with her. "So prim and proper. The real English Miss. Don't think that pretty accent will cut the ice with the big boys when they try to — well, when things get hot. My advice to you, Miss Ellen J.," and he grasped the hand that was about to lift the bagel to her mouth, "is get out while the going's good, before you're burned."

"Why I . . . " But Ellen found that whatever clever retort she'd planned melted away before the concern in his eyes. There was also the touch of his fingers on her skin, which was doing unbearable things to her heart rate.

As if he, too, had been affected, he removed his hand and scooped up his journal, putting it into his briefcase. He slid on tinted glasses, stood up, and slung his jacket casually over his shoulder. "Think about what I said now. And I don't suppose you'll have to bribe Joe either to get my phone number, if you ever need my — "

"Thanks. It won't be necessary," she

told him calmly, although her interior was churning wildly. "But thanks again. And have a — "

"Nice day," he finished for her, grinning. "You too."

2

FORTUNATELY Ellen had little time to dwell on her encounter with Don Redman next few days. The death of a major international leader caused great flurries of activity on the world's money markets, and those at Geiger Associates, like everyone else in the financial world, moved at high speed to keep up with fluctuations, buying and selling frenziedly.

At last things began to settle down, and Ellen was able to draw breath. She hardly dared believe she had done well, but she was delighted that she had been able to survive the most feverish market she'd yet encountered.

"With everything relatively normal now," she said to Maggie, "it feels positively quiet, flat. It's incredibly exhilarating, isn't it?"

"That's one of the reasons we're

hooked on this career. It's a kind of addiction — the highs, the lows. We wouldn't last five minutes in any job without them."

Ellen nodded. "You're right. I wonder why people thought that it was a sensation only men could appreciate, up until now?"

Maggie flashed one of her brilliant, intense smiles. She was wearing a new, deeper red lipstick which accentuated her strong colouring — black hair, pale skin, vivid blue eyes.

"Kid, if I knew the answer to that one the world would have changed a long time ago. Maybe men wanted to keep all the fun to themselves."

"Maybe. Although according to one man I met, women simply aren't capable of appreciating or handling work like this. Or at least," she amended fairly, "he thinks *I'm* not."

"Oh yeah? He thinks you can't hack it? Bring him here one day, and he'll soon see how wrong he is — I bet he wouldn't be able to keep up."

"I'm afraid he would, though. Anyway, little chance of that," Ellen said, surprising herself with a sudden jab of sadness. "We didn't part on the best of terms, so I doubt I'll have to hear any more of his advice about getting back to England before I'm sent there."

Maggie's eyebrows shot up. "Wow. You mean he's so keen on you that he wants you to leave New York?"

Ellen gave a short laugh. "I hadn't thought of it like that. It sounds as if I made a direct mis-hit."

"He must have some saving graces, this guy, otherwise you wouldn't have stayed long enough to hear his insults — and remember them."

"He's very, very attractive. And full of physical energy."

"Just his personality that stinks?"

"Um — no. Only he doesn't understand that — "

Ellen broke off as her name was barked out behind her. "Huntsworth, when you've finished gossiping please?" She turned, annoyed that Abrams had caught her talking about a man with Maggie, but he gave no indication that he had overheard. As usual, it was impossible to guess his inner thoughts.

"You the one responsible for this Jap deal?" he said, waving a piece of paper Ellen recognised.

She steeled herself looked him coolly in the eye. "That's right," she acknowledged. "Any problems?"

His hard brown eyes behind thick-lensed glasses did not waver. "You used the wrong forms. The paperwork's been returned."

Ellen's heart sank. Surely the deal wouldn't fall through because of faulty administration? It was the first time she'd handled a transaction of this nature and complexity at Geiger, and she'd had to ask for Mark's help as Maggie wasn't around. Ellen realised she must have misunderstood his instructions.

She stood her ground, however, and managed to stop herself from apologising or blaming herself — yet. That sort of self-recrimination might well be seen as a sign of weakness — especially by someone like Abrams.

"If the deal's still on," she said, "can you direct me on the paperwork?"

Abrams gave a sharp shake of his head, and Ellen's heart now reached the tip of her shoes, but at his next words all her confidence was restored.

"Karen's doing it. It's OK, you're still green on this one." He turned to go, then said over his shoulder, "You must have handled it OK. The Japs said they were impressed."

When he was out of earshot Maggie gripped Ellen's arm and squeezed it. "Hey, that's great. The Japanese expect the best."

"I'm glad they didn't drop the deal. Abrams seemed pleased, too. I thought he might still be holding a grudge against me for the other day, but instead he's trying to help me out."

"Maybe yes, maybe no," Maggie said cryptically. "You must have researched that portfolio well for him, and that would have given him an easy ride.

Besides, he couldn't let this big deal slip or Geiger would hear of it. Abrams'll consider you both quits now." She looked down at some papers in front of her, then asked, without looking at Ellen, "Was it Abrams who actually took you on?"

"You know I worked in Geiger's London office. I was selected and interviewed there — and it was Geiger who signed my letter of acceptance. Why?"

Maggie shrugged. "Just curious. But if you're a choice of the Great Man himself, you'd better get back to your vid!"

When she sat down again Ellen saw, written on a sheet of paper in large capitals, "Congratulations! Mark." She looked up, grinned, and waved to him.

Ellen was sitting at the circular smoked glass table in one corner of her small living-eating-and-everything-room. Scattered across it were pamphlets, books, financial newspapers, a computer printout, and notebooks. She was trying to work, to keep abreast of her field, to live, breathe and eat figures, as Don put it, but the heat was making her lethargic. The sky outside was a lurid yellow-grey, the air felt steamy with July's humidity, and the high temperature was oppressive. Even the air-conditioning, efficient though it was, couldn't disguise the fact. Ellen longed for a thunderstorm to clear the air.

There was another reason for her inability to concentrate. Above her, separated by only a matter of a few yards, was Don Redman. Of course, he might not be in at that precise moment, but he would at some time be there, although, oddly, she hadn't bumped into him again this past week. She wanted to see him, and yet she didn't. The last thing she wanted was for him to take pity on her. He seemed to view her as a problem case, someone to be sorted out and gently placed on the right track. His track, of course.

She found herself wondering about him at various times. She wondered which of his parents was American, why he'd chosen to live in the States rather than England, what his job was — everything, in fact, about him. She also caught a key question popping into her mind, and brusquely shoved it out again. Was he married? He didn't wear a ring, but that meant nothing. And, if not married, surely there must be a girl friend somewhere about. This was not an attractive idea, but she couldn't see how such a personable man could be on the loose. It would be against nature's laws!

Ellen sighed. There didn't seem to be any way in which they could meet again, anyway. She had turned down his offer of help in no uncertain terms. Most of her girl friends would chide her for making such a mistake, but it would be wrong to meet him on false pretences, Ellen knew.

However, everything had changed a great deal since she'd cast off her shroud of self-pity. She felt she was definitely beginning to shape a new life here in New York, and things couldn't be going better at work, and now the ice there had been broken with at least one of her colleagues. She was meeting Maggie on Sunday and had planned a sight-seeing trip for herself on Saturday.

That meant she would, at last, be able to write a proper letter home. So far she hadn't dared, in case she inadvertantly let slip something of her homesickness, her trepidation at what she'd done. Her parents were kind, and they loved her, but if she showed the slightest chink in her armour, they would probably begin to plead with her to return home, piling on the pressure to back out now before disaster struck. Ellen couldn't imagine what sort of dreadful future they envisaged for her — she only knew they worried.

She steeled herself yet again against them. She would never give in. And that quadrupled the importance for her to resist Don Redman's advice, and for her to succeed alone.

The telephone rang. As she picked it up

a peculiar emotion prickled through her, which she recognised to her disgust as eager anticipation. She was hoping that it would be Don! Instead, she heard an unfamiliar, older woman's voice.

"Is that Ellen? You won't recognise my voice, but it's Aunt Theresa."

"But — aren't you in — "

"I was, dear, I was, but I'm right here in New York now. Todd has business here, and we're staying for three weeks."

Aunt Theresa's accent was a blend of Derbyshire and Mid-western twang. She had emigrated to the States with her husband soon after marriage, and Ellen had only met her twice when she was a small girl.

"Jennifer — your mum — gave me your address, and asked me to look out for you. I guess she thought as we were in the same country I could do it, though what she expected me to do from Florida, I don't know."

Ellen's heart sank. Why couldn't her mother leave well alone? She would have contacted her aunt in due course, perhaps visited her. Aunt Theresa and Uncle Todd might have made their way specially to New York to see her! The mention of 'business' might just be a cover. They might try to interfere . . .

"That's very kind of you, and it's lovely to hear from you. I'm fine, I really am."

"Of course you are, a bright young woman like you. But we would both love to see you. We've never had a chance to get to know each other, have we, and there'll be so much news to catch up on."

"Of course." Ellen tried to force cheerfulness into her voice. It wasn't Aunt Theresa's fault that Ellen wanted to be free of her family for now. "Perhaps we could meet — "

"Exactly. And it's all arranged," her aunt said energetically. "We're having a small party of friends here at our hotel suite tomorrow evening. Can you come?"

After making the arrangements Ellen slowly replaced the receiver and tried to feel pleased. She had been only ten when Uncle Todd and Aunt Theresa, her father's elder sister, had last come to England. She remembered little about them because at that age she had been out playing with friends most of the time. It probably would be fun to see them; as long as they didn't follow her mother's instructions too literally and try to take over her life.

As Ellen showered ready to go out the following evening her mind was full of the sights and sounds of her tourist's trip of the city. She had gazed up at glittering buildings, taken a horse-drawn carriage round Central Park, walked through art museums till her feet were sore, and knew that she had barely scratched the surface of what New York had to offer.

Ellen dusted sweet-smelling powder on her skin, stepped on the scales and was pleased to see her weight remained the same, then went to the wardrobe to choose her outfit for the party. A sober and sensible suit, the sort of thing she would wear to work, seemed to be the answer to a gathering of her aunt and uncle's old friends. Her black suit, with its pencil-slim skirt and fitted jacket, with a white blouse, were flattering to her figure. Shimmery golden-brown eye make-up accentuated her brown eyes, and she let her rich auburn hair lie loose and smooth to her shoulders.

The air was so sticky that she didn't bother to take a coat. As she left the building she wished for a fleeting second that Don Redman had been coming in, to see how smart she could look.

Her aunt and uncle were staying at the International Hotel, just within walking distance. She could always get a cab if she tried, but for now it was pleasanter to be outdoors on the sultry May evening.

The heat penetrated quickly to her skin. The sky was hazy, a sickly yellow, and she was glad when a wind sprang up. But some moments later she noticed it began to grow darker and looked up to see black clouds spreading above the tall buildings. A low, ominous rumble of thunder speeded her steps, and she began to look over her shoulder for a cab.

When large, heavy drops of rain began to spatter the pavement Ellen broke into a near-run. Every cab was either occupied or had its light out, and she had no idea what bus to take. Around her the crowds began to take cover, but she kept gamely on. It couldn't be far now, although somehow what had looked a reasonable walk on the map had expanded in reality. Perhaps it would be only a short, sharp shower, Ellen was thinking, when the heavens opened, and she was caught crossing the road. By the time she had reached the next possible shelter she was already drenched. She could not get any wetter.

Five minutes later Ellen arrived at the hotel. Her shoes squelched and she had lost a buckle from one of them. She caught a glimpse of herself in some mirrored tiles. She looked like a drowned rat, she thought. Chin up, she swallowed the lump of frustration in her throat and made her way up to the third floor, where she paused to straighten her clothes as best she could outside her aunt's door.

Then, as she reached out to knock, a tanned, male hand beat her to it, clasped her fingers in his, and brought them down again.

"So this was one eventuality you didn't foresee, Miss Ellen J?"

Ellen, with as much dignity as she could muster, met Don Redman's humorous gaze. He stood leaning against the door frame with one arm, the other still holding her hand, looking her up and down. Ellen's heart bumped in her chest as she took in again the thick black hair with those unusual flecks of grey, the wide, sensual mouth, the clear grey eyes. Only a few raindrops beaded his jacket. Then she remembered her own condition — soaked to the skin, hair plastered to her head, she must be completely unappealing.

"That was a terrible thunderstorm, took me completely by surprise. I've never been so wet before in my . . ." Ellen trailed off, thinking, 'Oh no — here

I go, talking about the weather again.' "I see you didn't make my mistake."

"I got a cab — if I'd known you were coming here, I'd've shared it with you. Didn't you want to take one?"

She shook her head. "I tried, but I couldn't get one to stop," she confessed.

Don shook her hand gently. "Lesson Number Two — ask Joe. That's what he's for, partly. OK?"

As his eyes roamed over her Ellen suddenly realised her wet blouse was almost transparent, revealing the outline of the shell-pink bra she was wearing. Quickly she held her jacket up in front of her, and was rewarded with a broad smile.

"Don't worry on my account — I'm not easily shockable!"

Ellen grimaced. "Will you let me knock or ring now, please? I could die of pneumonia standing out here."

"Of course," he released her instantly, and pressed the doorbell. "I didn't realise you were cold."

Ellen gave a rueful smile. "Too pleased

about catching me out again, I suppose. Well, you needn't wait, my aunt'll be answering the door any second now."

"That's OK. I'm happy to wait with you."

"That's very polite. But I warn you, fairly, this little incident isn't a defeat, merely a small setback."

But before Don could reply the door opened, and Ellen was enveloped in her Aunt Theresa's instant concern. "Oh, you poor thing, you're soaking. It is Ellen, isn't it? You haven't changed that much." Then, to Ellen's amazement, she went on, in a warmly affectionate tone, "Good evening Don, lovely to see you. I see you're nice and dry." They kissed each other on the cheek, then Aunt Theresa directed him towards an inner room where there was the chatter and clinking of glasses from guests already arrived. Don cast Ellen an amused glance over his shoulder, while she shook her head at him.

Aunt Theresa didn't give Ellen the

chance to ask why Don was at her party as she plied her with questions about the family, and steered her across the ante-room into the master bedroom. Aunt Theresa was resplendant in a full-length multi-coloured gown, her grey hair tinted and elegantly set, her skin tanned a golden brown.

"While you dry off in the bathroom I'll look through your cousin Selena's clothes in the other bedroom. She's about your size."

Ellen stared at her face in the bathroom mirror in dismay. Her nose was pink and her mascara was smudged where she'd wiped the rain out of her eyes. Quickly she restored herself with hairdrier and her aunt's make-up to an only slightly damp version of her former glory. Then, wrapped in a towel, joined her aunt.

"You look lovely — just like your mother when my brother was courting her. Now, here's a dress of Selena's for you — unfortunately she can't be here this evening."

Ellen slid on the silvery dress. It fitted

her almost like a second skin. It had narrow straps, and left what, to Ellen's eyes, was a vast expanse of skin bare at both front and back. She could feel the air circulating over her creamy flesh.

"I can't wear this!" she gasped involuntarily.

"Why ever not? It looks wonderful on you, and it goes well with your hair." Aunt Theresa brushed her objections aside and led her towards the party. Before they went in Ellen paused and asked the question which had been burning inside her. "How do you know Don Redman?"

"Don? He's Todd's stockbroker, and he's brilliant — just about the best. We're so lucky to have him. Todd sold off his engineering firm a couple of years ago you remember? — and we went to live in Florida, good for my arthritis, and we live off the investments. It wasn't a huge amount he got — it was only a small company — but Don achieves fantastic things for us."

Ellen tried to digest the news that Don

had not only kept this information from her when she had told him about her own job, but that he was a rival. She found that she couldn't even swallow it, let alone digest it.

Ellen had expected her aunt and uncle's gathering of friends to be a polite, perhaps even staid, affair. Instead she found about thirty people of all ages, with more arriving, all talking and laughing, with music playing in the background. She felt less shy and conspicuous once she began chatting too, and had seen other, similar dresses. She particularly liked a slinky cream dress worn by a woman a few years older than Ellen with abundant red hair. She wasn't surprised to see Don join her and embark on an intimate conversation that involved them touching each others' hands, and putting their heads so close their hair mingled, red against black.

Ellen turned her back on Don and put everything she could into meeting the people her aunt and uncle introduced. Soon she was enjoying herself very much — even though the thought of Don somewhere in the room behind her caused an uneasy itchy sensation on her skin.

Later, Ellen found herself momentarily alone. She walked to the window, where the curtains were not yet drawn, and looked out. It was still raining, the drops cascading down the glass in rivulets, making the scene outside runny, like an Impressionist painting. She could just make out a soundless flash of lightning on the horizon, filling the dark sky with ripples of light.

"That dress is quite stunning," said a voice behind her. "Are you sure you didn't arrange to get wet so that you could startle everyone, like Cinderella?"

Ellen looked at Don's faint reflection in the window. She was just getting used to the dress, but now Don's eyes seemed to make her aware all over again of her bare shoulders.

"You've got it wrong," she said. "This is me as the pumpkin. Just wait and see what happens at midnight!"

"What an invitation! So this is the hidden, unfettered Miss Huntsworth. Do you have further surprises in store?"

"This was my aunt's idea, not mine," Ellen replied, "so I can't claim it as a new image."

"Ah, wasn't I playing fair — not cricket?" And he assumed a pure English accent. "Unfortunately, I always play to win — and I don't hide the fact. That's my American half coming out. Do you know how to play to win?"

Ellen looked up at him. Tonight Don seemed different, more dangerous. "A woman can be as competitive as a man, I think. It depends what the stakes are. Some aren't worth it."

"Where's that sense of adventure gone? Has something happened to make you change your mind already about our great city? Or is it your job? You can be level with me, Ellen. I've no axe to grind."

"On the contrary, everything's just great, and I'm very happy. As for being on the level — why didn't you tell me you were in the same business as me — and one of the best, too, by all accounts?"

He gave a mock sigh. "OK, who's been talking — your Aunt Theresa, I guess. Understandable in the circumstances."

"But why keep it a secret — did you think I'd try to use you?"

His surprise was genuine. "Gracious, no. Haven't I offered you my help? It just . . . didn't seem relevant."

"Not relevant! How naive I must've sounded."

"I can tell you're mad at me. No, not naïve — maybe a mite idealistic, and nothing wrong with that — except you'll have to forget it in our world."

"Idealistic," Ellen repeated sadly. "Is that a dirty word around here?"

"Hey now, no need to look so serious. Nothing wrong with idealism — in its place."

"Well, I might just prove you wrong. I'd rather be unsophisticated than ruthless. What do you say to that?"

"I'd say you were biting off more

than you can chew." Don's eyes had darkened into unfathomable depths, and Ellen was finding it harder and harder to concentrate on their conversation. If only he wouldn't stand so close to her, so that she found it difficult to breathe. "That's some challenge you're throwing out there. I'm beginning to think the little Miss in her neat suits is just a clever decoy."

In her heart of hearts Ellen knew that she might very well turn out to be nothing more than a little Miss, unsophisticated, lacking the guts that were necessary . . . although if she failed, at least she'd know she'd tried, very hard. But she couldn't reveal any of this to Don, not now. He would only want to come to her rescue once more, although she wasn't sure she felt safer with that Don than with this demanding, very male, man.

Ellen squared her shoulders. "It's a challenge I intend to follow through. So you'd better watch out!"

Don's mouth twitched. "Oh, I will, I

will," he murmured.

"Now you're humouring me — or have you been deliberately leading me on?"

"Not guilty, I promise." Don held up his hands in mock surrender, and Ellen, with an exasperated noise, tried to push past him, but suddenly his hand was at her waist, and he was drawing her towards him. "Understand me, Ellen, I just don't want any harm to come to you. Now, they seem to be playing our tune. Don't rush off."

And then she was in his arms, her flushed cheek resting against his shoulder. She heard his voice from far away say, "Maybe I should've said 'Please allow me the pleasure of this dance' but by the time I'd've got the words out, you'd've escaped. You see, I don't play fair."

Ellen found it impossible to answer him. Round his shoulder she could make out their reflection in the rain-streaked window. Behind them a few other couples were also dancing to the slow melody, and the lights were dimmed.

Ellen soon discovered that Don did not play fair. His hand, firm and experienced, moved down the flare of her hip, and she could feel its warmth through the thin material of her dress. Their bodies seemed to fit perfectly together, curve for curve. The roughness of his suit was oddly pleasant against her bare skin, and she could smell the mingled scent of his aftershave, his skin, his hair. And she might have imagined it, but she was sure she felt the faint brush of his lips along her shoulder . . .

No, Don wasn't playing fair. He must have guessed what his physical presence did to her, and was deliberately using it to ensure that she didn't get away from him. The trouble was, she liked it. Too much. But she couldn't shake off the suspicion that Don was using this moment as a weapon to weaken her resolve.

As they moved round she could see her aunt across the room, and that firmed her shaking will. What would she think of her niece's abandoned behaviour? As the music finished she pulled away from Don.

"Thank you," she said firmly, "but I really mustn't monopolise you." And with a dazzling smile she walked away. She didn't look back. If she had, she would have been astonished at the satisfied smile on his face.

Soon the party began to break up as people left to go out to supper or go on to a show. Ellen's clothes were still damp, and she knew she'd have to wear the silvery dress home.

"We'll order you a taxi," said Aunt Theresa. "Selena won't mind about that dress, and we'll be seeing you again soon, and she'll be with us then." She gave Ellen's hand an affectionate squeeze. "I'll be able to tell your father and mother how well you're settling in. I'm sure it'll put their minds at rest."

"You know they didn't want me to come?" Ellen asked.

Tactfully her aunt didn't try to take sides. "They must love you very much," was all she said, then, "Oh, Don's leaving now — didn't you tell me you both lived in the same apartment building? Perhaps you could share a taxi with him." And she was gone before Ellen could stop her.

"Of course Ellen can come with me. I'll see her safely home," she heard Don say. "Is she ready now?"

As Ellen approached her emotions were pulling her in two directions. She wanted to be with him, but she didn't trust herself in his company. But then the question was resolved for her. The redhead with whom he'd been talking earlier slid her arm through his. "Ready to go when you are," she said cheerfully, with a friendly smile.

"I can see you're going to have quite an escort. Two lovely girls," said Ellen's uncle.

"I'd rather stay on here for a little," Ellen interrupted. "We've got so much to talk about. But thank you all the same." And she smiled sweetly at Don, who merely nodded casually.

"As you like," he said, leaving Ellen fuming. What did she care?

3

IT was hot, hot and humid. Somewhere up above, through the layer of haze and city fumes, was a blue sky, but it looked a pale yellow colour from where Ellen was standing. The brassy sun glinted off those skyscraper windows which weren't tinted; and at ground level, with the traffic angrily nose to tail, the air was heavy and stifling. Ellen stepped through the large, plate-glass doors of the Pepper Building, into the relief of the cool, air-conditioned lobby and strode smartly over to the bank of elevators, each going to a different section of floors. She stepped into the one destined for the fourteenth floor, closely hemmed in as usual by other, equally hot individuals, each waiting impatiently to be released to their place of work. After just a few weeks her journey was quite familiar, and Ellen was able to get through it on auto-pilot, snapping fully awake as she entered Geiger Associates' suite of offices.

"Ellen — hi — have a good weekend?"

Maggie had stopped in reception to speak with Yolande, the receptionist, who presided over a splendid, deeply-carpeted area, filled with leafy green plants under special lighting, original lithographs on the walls, and deep low settees and armchairs. "Hi — looks like I almost beat you to it today."

Maggie grimaced. "The faucet stuck, I wrenched it, it came on — then wouldn't turn off. I had to call in maintenance." She rolled her eyes. "If it wasn't impossible to find another place to live in Manhattan these days I'd move from that dump — bye for now Yolande — but what can you do?"

"I like it." Ellen defended Maggie's apartment in a brownstone co-op building on the Upper West side. It had polished wooden floorboards and was laid out in a haphazard way, and had a fire escape doubling as a balcony at the back. Maggie had furnished it in bright, African style patterns. "More character than mine, bigger, and at least you can open some of your windows."

"Feeling cooped up? I know about that too well." They began to stroll along the corridor to the stockbrokers' room. "If I only had a friend who lived out on Long Island, or anywhere on the coast."

Ellen smiled. "The seaside. Lovely! But in fact I had a busy Saturday, sightseeing around town, and then a party — my aunt and uncle from Florida are in town. And you'll never guess who I met there."

"Who?" Maggie's quick movement of her head and the gleam in her eyes encouraged Ellen to go on.

"That man I told you about, the one who keeps trying to persuade me to go back home to England. He's in the financial business too."

"And he never told you? It sounds as if he's got a chip on his shoulder about women in the Stock Market. Or perhaps he's insecure."

63

"Don Redman? No I don't think so. In fact I — " Ellen broke off as Maggie's eyes widened in surprise, and Mark, who was passing on his way to the cold drinks machine, paused and said, "Redman? What's new now?"

"Why? What's this all about? Have you both heard of him?" Ellen looked from Maggie to Mark in bewilderment.

"Sure, who hasn't? When Redman moves, everyone follows suit. Smart isn't in it. It's like he's got some sort of sixth sense," Mark told her.

"He's honest too," Maggie added. "No one's ever hinted at double dealing. And he's very, very rich."

"Wouldn't we all like to be so lucky." Mark gave a mock sigh.

"Of course, they say he's married to his computer, and takes figures to bed with him. Sorry, Ellen, it sounds as if he's a hopeless case," Maggie said sympathetically.

Mark's amused glance caught Ellen's eye. "Has our English cousin fallen for Redman? I'm afraid Maggie's right, that guy's got a dollar sign engraved on his heart."

"I haven't fallen for him," Ellen denied. "He just happens to think he can tell me how to run my life."

Mark laid a hand on her arm. "Glad to hear it. Keep your heart your own where he's concerned and you'll be safe. Why not play along with him for what you can get? Some women would."

Ellen shook her head. "Not my style."

Yolande called up the corridor, "Maggie, your phone's on hold."

"Here we go — " Maggie's chin set determinedly and she headed for her desk at a run.

"Want a drink?" Mark asked Ellen.

"Love one — lemonade."

Ellen sat down and pulled her notes towards her, switched on her computer terminals, and began to prepare herself for work in a light-hearted frame of mind. Heartened by Mark's friendliness, she hoped it would only be a matter of time before the others thawed too and began to accept her. Perhaps it was partly in her imagination.

The comments about Don, though, had bitten deep. Maggie had said he was honest, and she'd go along with that, but it seemed he was even more of a financial superstar than she'd thought. He hadn't tried in any way to flaunt his riches, or to parade his status. It would have added weight to his arguments to point out exactly how experienced he was in the financial field.

But could his obsession with money be the explanation for his opposition to her? Did he think that such an important thing should be in the hands of someone older, that she was too naïve and frivolous?

If they met again she determined she would keep to herself what she had learned. It was clearly something he wanted to reveal when he was ready. Don seemed to be a man of mystery. But it wasn't mysterious that his touch did strange things to her, threatened to make her lose control. At least her heart was still safely her own, as she'd told Mark and Maggie.

The market was frenetic that day. One big business was trying to take over another, and while a lot of people were paying all their attention to that, Ellen was busy buying and selling in a different area, notching up some pleasing profits. She was so busy that she didn't immediately read the memo that arrived from Abrams, and when she did it was only just in time. It announced that he was passing on a new, small client to her, who was already on his way to see her. Almost straight away Yolande rang through to tell her that Mr. Renkovic was in reception.

He had thick, iron-grey hair that stood up like a brush, and he chewed on the end of a cigar, not lighting it because their office was a no smoking zone. He was moving from another stockbroker to Geigers, and Ellen didn't mind talking to him at all — what did rankle with her was the way that Abrams had put 'as you handle mainly small clients, Mr.

Renkovic will be suitable for you'. The implication was that she was strictly small time. Yet Abrams knew that she handled several large institutions, too.

She didn't betray any of this inter-office wrangling to Mr. Renkovic, but welcomed him and supplied him with tea.

"See," he told her straight away, "I've got this weak heart. I can't work and I can't handle excitement. But I got medical insurance. You got medical insurance?" Ellen nodded. It was something she had been advised to do when coming to America. "Well, make sure it's a good one. Mine paid out, so I can invest, live on the income. How d'you like that? But my last broker, he was nuts, put it all in Eurobonds. Nuts!"

Ellen, who'd been privately very impressed with Eurobonds, smiled and leaned forward, about to explain their performance, but before she could begin he too leaned forward and said confidentially, "See, it's not just for me, it's for my mother too, she's nearly ninety and I take care of her, know what I mean?"

"I promise you, Mr. Renkovic, your money's in safe hands. I'll do all I can for you."

"You're English aren't you — or is it Australian? Never could tell the difference. But I like that. Now, I'm not as dumb as I look. I read the papers, I watch television. I've got some suggestions for you — I mean, I'd do it myself, but I've got this weak heart. Mustn't get upset, see?"

Ellen spent longer than she could really afford steering Mr. Renkovic away from the very risky investments he favoured towards safer waters which would be suitable for the regular income he needed. In the end they reached a compromise, and Ellen saw him out. On the way back she bumped into Mark.

"Hey," he grinned, "you look whacked — and I know why."

"Why?"

"Just one word — Renkovic!"

"You've seen him before?" Ellen asked in surprise.

"Everyone's seen him before. He

changes brokers as regularly as his socks, or nearly. He gets hare-brained ideas, insists you do what he wants, then complains when he loses money. I don't know why he uses a stockbroker."

"He was telling me about his medical condition, a weak — "

"Not that old story, the weak heart. Don't believe a word of it. He's strong as a horse. No one's been able to handle him. How did he come to you?"

Ellen smiled wearily. "My good friend Mr. Abrams thought I was just the person for him."

"Abrams — I'm surprised he let Mr. Renkovic in through the door. I'm certain he's been here before."

"The way Mr. Abrams feels about me he probably invited Mr. Renkovic in specially for me! I thought I'd made an enemy of him, then it all seemed to blow over, but not so I see now. I wonder why, though?"

"Like that is it? No one's been able to figure out what makes Abrams tick. Say, you need a break. Let's have a drink

70

together one evening, off load all our troubles on each other's shoulders."

"I'd love to — although I think I'll be doing most of the off loading. I'm going to be busy most of this week with relatives, but what about the weekend?"

"That'll be great. I know a bar that puts the Four Seasons in the shade. You'll love it," Mark said confidently.

Feeling buoyed up by Mark's friendly invitation, and secure in the knowledge that she had a good friend in Maggie, Ellen's initial loneliness evaporated, and she counted herself very lucky. She also floated though the evenings in the company of her new-found aunt and uncle and cousin, simply enjoying being with them, with the added bonus that they wanted to see all the new shows at the theatre, the ballet, and knew their way around the restaurants and clubs.

Her first paycheck was paid into the bank at the end of the month, and she spent every spare moment scrambling through the big department stores and the small, smart boutiques, on a spending spree that filled her wardrobe and drawers with neat clothes for work, some light summer wear for the months ahead, and some glamorous clothes too for the evening, which left her bank balance decidedly off-colour once she'd paid the rent.

All her earlier gloom and despondency had fled. Now she felt just like any other New Yorker, timing her day to precision, dashing from one appointment to the next, concentrating on her work for some twelve hours of the day, and then, during the long humid evenings, playing as hard as she could. She telephoned her parents, which reassured them further, and when her mother said that she was pleased to hear Ellen sounding so happy, it brought a lump to her throat.

There were no hitches now, she thought, as on Friday evening she snapped her files shut, turned off the VDUs, slipped papers into her desk drawers and locked them, and picked up her briefcase. Even Abrams had done nothing further to upset her that week. She and Mr. Renkovic were getting along together very well, and her other clients seemed happy too. No, this weekend she would be able to enjoy herself to the full, without any worries.

It was Aunt Theresa and Uncle Todd's last evening in New York, and they were meeting Ellen and Selena in the Russian Tea Rooms for a drink, before going on to eat at a famous fish restaurant, and then finishing off the evening at a jazz club. Ellen was looking forward to wearing the designer outfit she'd bought the day before. A green patterned silk camisole top, baggy leggings that caught tight at the ankles, and a long jacket with pockets. She'd also splashed out on matching shoes.

On Saturday night she was seeing Mark for a drink. And, as for Don Redman . . . well, now she only thought of him every second second, and although she still looked automatically in Arnaldi's every time she passed, she no longer felt so disappointed at not seeing him in there, only a kind of dull ache.

On her way out of the quiet office she paused to glance at a notice board. As she did so she became aware that a man and a woman were talking in low voices together, screened by some green plants. She wouldn't normally have listened, but she heard her own name mentioned, and stood stock still in surprise.

"But I still can't see any justification for taking on this Huntsworth. I mean, what's her record? Nothing," the man was saying.

"I heard Geiger himself arranged it. The Old Man. So perhaps he knows . . . " the woman replied uncertainly.

"She has no right to be sitting in that chair. We all know that — and so do you, if you think about it," the man said forcefully.

"Maybe she won't last. I mean, if she really hasn't got the experience." The man laughed, a chilling sound. "Three months? Two? Want to take a bet on it?"

Cheeks burning red with indignation, Ellen thought, 'I'll survive a lot longer than either of you imagine — and you can freeze me out all you want, it won't make the slightest bit of difference.' She drew in a deep breath, ready to confront them, demand an explanation for the way in which they were talking about her, particularly the man. She knew perfectly well that it was they who lacked justification . . . and yet, it must have come from somewhere. Did they resent an English person taking an American job? But there were plenty of Americans working in the City of London. It made no sense to her at all.

But she'd hesistated a fraction of a second too long. An office door clicked to behind her, and out of the corner of her eye she saw Abrams walking towards her, his eyes like polished pebbles, boring into her. The last thing Ellen wanted was for him to overhear such a confrontation. It would only give him satisfaction. Besides, she didn't really like the idea of eavesdropping. How right it was that you never overheard good of yourself! She would let it rest for now; she nodded briefly towards Abrams, then headed quickly for the elevators, hoping not to get trapped in one with him.

Once safely on her way down, ahead of Abrams, she closed her eyes momentarily, still stinging from the cruel remarks she'd heard. Perhaps Mark would be able to throw light on what was going on. Maggie had been sympathetic, but had been doubtful about Ellen's claim, and had suggested it might be Ellen feeling new and strange. But then Maggie had only been at Geigers a few weeks longer than Ellen. Ellen was glad that Maggie wasn't included in the cold treatment for talking to Ellen. And now she had definite proof.

As if to refute what she'd heard she took especial care when preparing to go out that evening. After a tepid shower to cool off she let the green silk top slide over her shoulders, fastened the high waist of the trousers, and brushed her hair till it shone before catching it with combs so that one side was pulled away from her face while the other fell in auburn waves. Although she couldn't entirely shake off what she'd heard, she made a determined effort to put it out of her mind. She knew she was in the right, and she had to cling to that sane thought.

The Russian Tea Rooms, practically next door to the Carnegie Hall and opposite Central Park, looked unostentatious from the outside. Inside, however, it was an expanse of snowy white clothed tables reflected in bright mirrors along the walls, waiters in Russian style shirts and waistcoats. There was only a sprinkling of customers at this hour of the day.

As the receptionist was taking her name, a familiar voice said behind her, "I'll show Miss Huntsworth to her table, Tanya," and he touched her arm.

The receptionist smiled meltingly. "Thank you, Mr. Redman."

Trying to calm her racing heart Ellen said, "So this is where you eat when Arnaldi's is full!"

Don grinned down at her. "I can tell

you, they don't have anything to match the Special. It'd be unfair to ask you if you finished it all."

"I certainly didn't need to eat again for a long time." As Ellen spoke she was acutely conscious of Don's hand resting lightly on her waist, escorting her to her uncle and aunt's table towards the back of the long room, and could feel his eyes appraising her. His smile had lit up his clear light grey eyes, and he seemed too warm, too alive to be the calculating machine that others had called him.

But then, what did she really know about him? A few facts, yes, but she realised he rarely betrayed what really went on behind that attractive exterior. Beneath that charm could lie all manner of secrets — and yet, despite that, she trusted him.

"And how are things at Geiger Associates?" he asked.

"Everything is great. I haven't plunged it or anyone else into financial ruin."

"Why ever should you? The capable Miss E. J. Huntsworth — but no, I've

78

been told not to give you any more lectures on the high risks you're taking."

Ellen stopped. They hadn't quite reached within earshot of her aunt and uncle's table.

"High risks?" she said patiently. "Of course it's high risk — but then don't you do the same thing a hundred times a day? Why should it be all right for you and not for me? Aunt Theresa told me you like to go sub aqua diving in the Caribbean, and that's infested with sharks!"

"That's different," Don replied, equally patiently. "I've studied sub aqua, I've been doing it for years, and I know all the dangers. I've trained to handle any circumstances."

"And so have I trained — but we both know it's only in practice that you can really learn. And so far the sharks of Wall Street haven't even got within nibbling range. Even if they did, it would be good — what do you mean, told not to lecture me?"

"Now listen to me. If I saw you

about to fall off a cliff, would you want me to stand silently by? No. As for 'told', your Aunt Theresa has a very persuasive manner — perhaps gently persuaded would be more accurate."

"I am not, repeat not, about to fall negligently off any cliffs, and I don't like the fact that you think I am. And exactly why were you discussing me with my aunt and uncle when I wasn't there to defend myself?"

"Discussing you — I wouldn't put it as strongly as that. It just so happened you came up in the course of the conversation."

"When you, I expect, were trying to explain to my aunt and uncle that you think me totally unsuitable for my job, for New York, and should be headed back for jolly England. Well, I'm glad that Aunt Theresa didn't believe you. At least I've got one champion."

"They're all your champions — and they're all sitting there wondering why we're so rudely ignoring them, and shouting at each other in loud whispers!

Don't you think you're over-reacting, especially when you've got the facts wrong?"

"Facts wrong? How can I when you told me yourself Aunt Theresa told you or persuaded you — not to lecture me. She must've known about it."

"In the first place, they asked me about you — natural family concern. And in the second place, it's time you cooled down and we joined them." He tucked a firm, commanding hand under her elbow and conducted her forward.

She fixed a smile on her face to hide her seething anger, and didn't allow a flicker to cross it when he hissed: "Remember, cool down. This is their last night. Do you want to spoil it?"

He was right, that was the last thing she wanted to do. When Aunt Theresa and Uncle Todd asked what they'd been arguing about, she laughed, and said, "Just a disagreement about some share prices," as if it was unimportant.

Somehow she managed to relax and

enter into the spirit of the evening. Don went with them to the restaurant, and she saw how skilful he was at making sure everyone felt part of the party. As they talked and laughed she began to think. Had she over-reacted? Had she been so bruised from those remarks she'd heard before leaving Geigers that the idea of anyone else — especially someone she'd really trusted, like Don — talking about her behind her back seemed insupportable? And of course what had happened under-lined exactly the sort of thing he'd been warning her about, which made it worse.

Selena's boyfriend Sammy had joined them for the meal too, his easy-going, affectionate nature and infectious laugh adding to the happy atmosphere. Selena looked stunning in the silvery dress that Ellen had borrowed, her taller figure suiting it better, though she was younger than Ellen. Her straight blonde hair she wore braided to one side in a thick plait, while Aunt Theresa's boldly patterned dress and tinted hair were both stylish and original, and all the men agreed they were the three most attractive women in New York.

Ellen's anger had almost melted away by the time Selena accompanied her to the powder room before leaving the restaurant. As soon as they were inside Selena burst out, eyes gleaming good-humouredly, "Ellen — what was that all about! Come clean now, I don't believe for a second you were discussing share prices!"

"Well — maybe you're right. I was a bit upset, I think; you know, Friday night, and when Don said he'd been discussing me with Auntie I just flared up. He seems to think I'm incapable of looking after myself, and that's what he was telling Aunt Theresa."

"I didn't know — oh, wait a minute, I was there. But it wasn't like that. Mom and Pop asked how you were getting along — they're very proud of you — and Don said he guessed you weren't likely to tell him, 'cause he'd given you too much unwanted advice already, so Mom said why not leave you to it — or words to that effect."

"I see," Ellen said slowly. "Sounds like I got it wrong — no wonder Don was telling me to cool down."

"Reconciliation, that's what you two need. And I know just — "

Ellen grinned. "Thanks, but I'd better apologise my own way."

She wasn't given the chance that evening. As they all left the restaurant Don said goodbye. He wasn't accompanying them to the nightclub. He gave nothing away as they said goodbye, but Ellen hated the idea of parting from Don on such bad terms, and was in danger of brooding about it the rest of the evening.

She'd blithely assured Mark her heart was still her own. But it felt now that she'd been very, very wrong.

"Yes, Mrs Goldberg, I'll do what I can to help you. Would you like me to send the information over?"

"Yes please, if you would. You know I

have these terrible dreams, that I've lost all my money."

"Then you needn't worry any more. It's all perfectly safe."

Ellen had soon discovered that Mrs. Goldberg's almost daily calls were due to loneliness. She found herself enjoying talking to her between dealing with her bigger clients. No sooner had she rung off, however, than Mr. Renkovic was on the phone.

"You got to do what I say," he began without preamble. "I've been studying this whole thing for a long time now, and I've got a real hunch. I know where the money's to be made. You got to go for metals."

"Metals! But Mr. Renkovic — "

"I've been around, you know. I know what I'm talking about."

"I'm sure you do," she said, "but have you thought of this?" And she rattled off some facts and figures and percentages, flicking queries into the computer as she went, receiving instantaneous answers.

"Hm. Maybe that's all so, but I really

feel this, you know . . . "

"I promise I'll keep an eye on metals. But at the moment, I don't think it would be a good idea."

"Well, I hear rumours, I get around you know."

"The rumours haven't reached me, and we've got one of the best analysis and research departments in town. But I'll investigate it for you."

"OK," he said cautiously, "I'll leave it with you but I'll call soon."

Ellen was relieved that she'd been able to talk Mr. Renkovic out of making any wild moves, but she was aware that this was only the first time. And what would happen if she were wrong and he was right? She'd look very silly then. The image of Don Redman floated into her mind, unbidden. "Have you got what it takes?" he was saying. "Yes I have," she muttered under her breath. And to do that she had to have faith in her own judgment.

All the same she asked Maggie when she was able, "What's happening to metals? Anything going on?"

Maggie, surprised, shrugged. "Nothing. Safe but dull. Why?"

"It's not important. It's just that — "

"Oh, here's Clyde. It's one of his specialities, let's ask him."

"No, I — it doesn't — " Ellen began, but Maggie had already halted the tall man and passed on Ellen's query.

"Metals?" he shook his head. "Absolutely nothing doing. Who wants to know?"

"Ellen here. She was wondering about rumours."

A smile spread across Clyde's face, and he began to laugh. "Well, Ellen, you've certainly got some strange ideas from somewhere. I guess England's just a bit behind the times with their training methods." And he went off, still chuckling.

"Sorry about that," Maggie said, raising her brows. "Why so insulting, I ask myself?"

Ellen shook her head. "I don't know. I told you before that I had the feeling that I wasn't welcome here, that some people wish I'd never arrived."

"Now listen to me," Maggie said firmly, "you're very welcome, especially with me. As for Clyde — you did scoop him the other day on that deal, didn't you?"

"I suppose so." But Ellen was unconvinced. Perhaps Clyde's had been the male voice she'd overheard on Friday? However, until she knew for sure who that had been, had recognised his voice without doubt, she decided to keep quiet about it.

"Hi, you two. Can anyone join the party?" Mark had sauntered over to join them. "Why so serious?"

"Ellen thinks something might be going to happen to metals."

Mark whistled. "First I've heard. You can pull a report on it, but I'd be very surprised. Where did you get this?"

"Mr. Renkovic," Ellen admitted reluctantly.

"Renkovic! Didn't I tell you that man has driven more stockbrokers crazy than he's had hot dinners?"

"I promised I'd find out for him, that's

all. You've persuaded me he's wrong. Now I just have to persuade him of that fact."

"He's always been wrong before, he can't possibly be right this time. Abrams knew what he was doing when he palmed him off on you. He's already wasting your time."

"You're right. Thanks Mark — you too, Maggie."

He slid an affectionate arm round her waist. "See you later, beautiful."

Ellen made her way back to her desk, deciding to forget Clyde's unpleasant remark. Having Mark's support as well as Maggie's was a bonus. He'd been a good companion when they'd gone out together on Saturday night. The bar he'd taken her to, dark wooden booths, plush red seats, low hanging lights with brass fittings, had created an intimate atmosphere, and on the walls were signed photographs of famous personalities who'd favoured the bar in the past. They'd talked non-stop about their work, about their training, about the differences between Wall Street and the City, then shared a taxi home, Ellen to be dropped off first.

"You're going to do well here in New York, I'm sure of it," Mark said, then added mischievously, "especially when you go round making such excellent contacts like Don Redman."

Although she'd enjoyed the evening, she had to admit to herself that there hadn't been many moments when Don Redman had not been in her thoughts. Always there was the knowledge that, amongst the teeming millions out there, there was one very special man who overshadowed all the rest.

"I struck lucky," she had smiled. "He happens to live in the same apartment block as me — right here, in fact."

"Had any working breakfasts yet?"

In the shadow of the cab's interior Ellen hoped Mark didn't see the colour flood her cheeks. "We had breakfast together one morning, but by accident, at the Deli next door."

"So he's not given you any tips?"

Ellen shook her head. "I've been given plenty of advice — but not the sort I want to take! Mark — I've really enjoyed this evening."

Mark had leaned forward and kissed her on the cheek, his arm around her shoulders, but had not tried to pull her closer. She was relieved that they both felt the same way — they wanted only friendship. He was pleasant company, classically good looking, but he produced none of the sparks in her that she experienced whenever Don was near.

Some time during the afternoon Karen, Abrams' secretary, came out with a tray of white envelopes and started to distribute them to each person. She only shook her head when asked what was going on. "Open and see for yourselves," was all she'd say. Towards the far side of the room Ellen and Maggie were almost the last to receive theirs and, judging by the exclamations of those who'd already read the contents, it wasn't good news.

Inside was a memo, signed by Mr. Geiger himself:

"I am pleased to announce that Geiger Associates is to merge with CZR, the financial management and other services consultancy, which will take effect as of now. There will of course be enormous benefits from being associated with such a large and successful company. It's to be anticipated that there will be the minimum of disruption to working arrangements, but you will be kept informed as and when developments occur."

So it had happened. The newspaper article Maggie had shown her had not been far wrong. A merger! But why? People began to gather in small knots around the room. Ellen joined Maggie and Mark, who were talking with Darryl and Shirlee.

"How can this happen?" Shirlee was demanding, tapping the paper with a long red fingernail. "We don't need this. We can go on without CZR."

"But think, with all that extra capital

and resources, just what we could achieve," Darryl disagreed.

"Maybe so — but this bit about the minimum of disruption. Can we be sure there won't be redundancies?" Maggie asked.

"Darryl could be right — maybe some reorganisation, but we could take on extra staff," Mark pointed out.

"I don't like it," Shirlee stuck to her guns. "Why has Geiger kept all this a secret from us — from everyone? I don't like the way he's handled it. The big question for me is — do I change my mind and accept that job offer I had a month ago?"

"I suppose we'll all have to decide whether to stay put and see what happens, or whether to look around for other jobs," Maggie said.

"There's one of us who probably won't have to worry about that anyway," Mark said suddenly.

They all looked at him. "Who's that?"

"Why, Ellen here. She's going to be sitting pretty."

"What do you mean?" Ellen asked in amazement. "I'm the newest, surely I'd be the first to go."

"Didn't you know? CZR is Don Redman's group — and you, Ellen, have already a friend and neighbour there, Don Redman himself. You couldn't be better placed if you tried."

4

ELLEN continued on automatic pilot for the rest of that and the following day. The whole office was subdued, and Ellen guessed that many, like her, although appearing calm and collected, were still trying to absorb the impact of the shock: Geigers was merging, was no longer independent, and their jobs might well have to change. There were plenty of differing opinions about what this would mean. Some people were optimistic, looking forward to new ideas, others were cautious, while others still were openly thinking about looking for new positions.

Ellen felt, she knew unreasonably, frustrated and upset. This was the job she'd come to America to do. Geiger himself had taken her on, or at least approved the appointment, wanting to bring a fresh approach into the stockbroking team. And it was Geiger Associates she'd felt proud to work for. She'd already built up a good relationship with her clients, and hoped that nothing would happen to disrupt that. She tried to count the benefits of being associated with a giant like CZR, with all its resources and expertise, but all she could think of was being swallowed up by a giant and becoming a very tiny, insignificant cog in the works of a huge machine.

Inevitably, all lines of thought led her back to the biggest stumbling block of all: Don Redman. She knew that she'd told him at some point that she worked for Geigers. And he hadn't breathed one word to her of what was about to happen. Of course, that was as it should be. He was supposed to keep quiet about the merger, or at least about the intricate details. But when she looked back over all their meetings she couldn't recall him giving the slightest hint of the negotiations that he was engaged in. No wonder he was called brilliant. It was as if he had a glittering surface that reflected probing eyes, giving nothing away of what was taking place inside.

She knew she had no right to have expected him to betray to her what was going on, especially as secrecy about the merger seemed so important. Unless — had his warning about New York's tough scene been a roundabout hint?

All that aside, the worst thing was that he would, in the future — perhaps even now — be working near her. At any moment he could stroll in and look over her shoulder, ask her questions about what she was doing. Or he could be looking at her file, along with everyone else's, discussing her merits — and demerits! — quite legitimately with Personnel. Or even with Abrams.

At this stage in her thinking she usually came to her sticking point. There was something she didn't want to face up to. But it was there, hardly put into words, and something she hadn't confided to anyone else. Ever since she'd come to the conclusion that Don meant more to her than a handsome thorn in the flesh, she'd suffered from a terrible disease — hope. Insane, reckless, quite without foundation, but there nevertheless. Hope that one day he might see her, not as someone wet behind the ears, a naïve, misty-eyed romantic, but as someone who could quicken his heart . . . Now that would be impossible.

She was an employee, a number, a statistic, a business problem, to him. He'd have to decide if she was cost-effective. Ugh. Hope was dead. Instead, there was the unbearable feeling that she could no longer meet him on equal terms, not now he was her boss.

And in the charged atmosphere of the stockbroker's office she could feel the increased hostility towards her. Gossip had quickly spread that she was 'in' with the new supremo, and now the hostility was fuelled by a new suspicion. Had she known about the merger before it happened? Was she, in fact — a spy for Don Redman?

Late one afternoon Abrams' secretary, Karen, buzzed through and asked her to come and see him straight away. Slowly she straightened her smart cream linen jacket and skirt, under which she wore a light turquoise T-shirt, just showing in the V of the jacket's neck; combed her hair, squared her shoulders, picked up her cream leather clutch bag, and walked towards his office, head held high. If this was the chop already, she was determined not to make his day by breaking down and crying.

Abrams looked hot and uncomfortable, his skin sheened with perspiration, the sleeves of his summer shirt flapping around his pale upper arms. He was looking very harassed. Ellen had only been in his office a few times, but normally his desk was neat and empty. Now every surface was cluttered with papers and files and computer printouts. She allowed herself an inward chuckle at the thought that Don had caused Abrams all these headaches.

"Huntsworth," Abrams said, his eyes

luminous behind his thick glasses, "you understand the full implications behind CZR's takeover, yes?"

Braced, Ellen nodded.

"OK. One of the chief executives is coming in to nose around. You're to do the showing, tomorrow, ten o'clock."

"Me? But I — I've been here such a short time," Ellen protested, taken aback. "I'm sure I don't know nearly enough about — "

"I don't have to remind you that you're the most junior around here. You know the office layout, don't you? OK, so just do it."

Ellen stood her ground. "Exactly how long is this guided tour supposed to take? An hour? Two?"

"You'll be at his disposal — and I use that word advisedly, so mark it — all day tomorrow, and from then on if he wants."

"But what about my clients?" Ellen gasped. "I can't just drop everything."

"Karen'll look after your phone for you, take messages. This is more important."

Ellen's cheeks turned a fiery red. Karen was very efficient, and she liked her, but to suggest that she could take over Ellen's chair just like that — it was impossible. She'd be able to do little more than take messages, and it also implied that Ellen's experience and expertise amounted to nothing.

"I disagree with you, Mr. Abrams," she said slowly, to avoid losing her temper. "It would be wrong of me to drop my work indefinitely, without proper organisation. Why not ask Karen to show the executive around?"

Abrams stared at her, and she felt the hairs on the back of her neck prickle. She was sure he was about to bawl her out. Instead he said, his voice softly menacing, "It's your choice, Huntsworth. Either you do as I say, or you know the kind of list your name will be at the top of, don't you? Either way, you won't be missed, got it?"

Ellen didn't like backing away from a fight, but this was one she could never win. It was do as he said or be recommended for firing or redundancy. She wasn't ready to face that, not yet. She'd have to back down for now, even if these were empty threats, but she smarted under the injustice of it. She managed a brief nod, then turned for the door.

"Be here at ten tomorrow then. And his name's Redman. Got it?"

Indignity heaped upon indignity. Abrams was determined to shake her confidence at every step, and now she had to contend with the fact that it was Don she'd be showing around. He would soon be able to find the holes in her knowledge. She managed a reassuring smile to Maggie and Mark to show that all was well, she hadn't been fired — yet.

Resolution firmed inside her. If Abrams hoped to force her to resign by his behaviour, she would prove him wrong. She would also do her best to show Don that he was wrong about her too. Tomorrow was going to be a tough day in all respects.

News of Ellen's assignment for the next day quickly spread, as she organised in a hurry to cover herself for not being at her desk. Ellen was aware that it made her position even more questionable to those of her colleagues who, for reasons still unknown to her, were hostile to her. They assumed that she'd engineered being with Don Redman for a day on purpose, pulling strings so that she could consolidate her position with him. Maggie and Mark were sympathetic, believing the truth. Mark was even optimistic.

"I wish it was me," he said. "Redman's opinion will count for as much, or more, than Mr. Geiger's. If you impress him, it'll count in your favour."

Ellen shook her head. "I wish it was you, too. For both our sakes. I suppose I ought to see it in terms of my career, but I can't. I thought I was ambitious, but I suppose that's not the whole story. And I don't know which way Don Redman'll take it — as a chance to find out my weak spots to prove that he was right all along about me not belonging here, or . . . I don't know."

"No need to worry," Maggie said briskly. "You'll be able to handle it. But you're right, Abrams has really got it in for you. You should be getting on with your job. If only there was some way you could complain about what he's doing."

"The trouble is he hasn't done anything concrete yet, it's all words," Mark said. "But whatever you do, Ellen, don't take it out on Redman — you must make a good impression on him. And put in a good word for your friends too," he added with a cheeky grin before moving off.

Ellen caught Maggie's eye and they both laughed. "Trust Mark to look on the bright side," Ellen said.

"He's like a boy sometimes. You have to watch your mothering instinct," Maggie said. "All that charm."

He was charming, yes, Ellen thought. But then Maggie had never come into contact with Don Redman's own devastating brand.

Ellen entered Abrams' office at ten precisely. Don had been sitting on a window sill, and he stood up when she came in. He was wearing a pale grey light suit, with matching shirt and shoes. His hair looked freshly washed, the grey flecks standing out against the shining black, and Ellen's heart lurched treacherously as he smiled and held out his hand in greeting.

"This is Ellen Huntsworth. She's your assistant for the day," Abrams was saying, "so if we'll just go over your itinerary once more — "

As Abrams talked Ellen was all the time conscious of Don standing only a few feet away, putting in the occasional, concise remark. Then at last they were released, and she was leading the way through the stockbrokers' room towards the special, executive lifts to take them down to the next floor and the special suite of offices that had been assigned to him. Although the frantic hum of voices didn't diminish one whit, Ellen knew that every eye was on them and, oddly, she wished she could shield him in some way from them.

"This is where I work," she explained, hoping that he would be distracted from realising he was the centre of attention. "As you can see, we have the very latest hardware, and the room's laid out to give us maximum privacy as well as easiest communication with each other."

"I see Ellen, thanks," Don said, glancing around, but without any great interest, and she realised, too late, that he'd be utterly familiar with all this. Then he surprised her by continuing, "Or should I call you Huntsworth? Is that just Abrams' way, or do you all call each other by your surnames — it's very old-fashioned." He paused. "I think I'll use Ellen anyway, if that's all right with you."

"I'd defend Geiger Associates about most things, but not that," she agreed. "Ellen's fine by me."

They got into the elevator, the doors closed, and they were alone together. It felt both very familiar to be with Don, and yet very strange, divided as they now were by their jobs. However, Ellen had already decided what she had to say to him, and the sooner she got on with it, the better.

"Mr. Redman," she began, only to be interrupted immediately.

"Don, please. You were quite happy to call me Don when you were spitting green fire at me the other day, so why go all formal on me now?"

She saw the flash of humour in his eyes, but persevered, praying that he wasn't going to make the apology any more difficult than it already was. "I'm glad you brought it up," she said awkwardly, "I wanted to talk to you about that — and something else too. You see, I — "

"What, two things you want to discuss with me already? It's going to be a lively day, I can tell."

Ellen compressed her lips, taken aback by Don's air of frivolity. This was supposed to be serious business. Then before she could speak he went on, "I guess one of the things you wanted to speak about was being reluctant to show me around. I can recognise an expression of resentment as well as the next man, so, if you're really going to protest about it, I'll have a word with Abrams."

Ellen herself would like to have several words with Abrams, preferably as unpleasant as possible, but then the implication of Don's words sank in and she said "No!" too loudly. She could feel Don's gaze scorching the top of her head. But if he told Abrams to let her off, Abrams would simply add it to his account against her. "No, that's not necessary," she said in a quieter voice, "but I think you should hear what I have to say."

"All right — but shall we go into the office first?"

Ellen realised that they were standing in the corridor outside the mahogany door of the visitor's suite, and led the way in. She began to describe the facilities, but trailed off as Don, after a quick glance at the dark wood-panelled room, the tasteful leather chesterfield and matching armchairs, the discreet smoked glass tables, rapidly seemed to lose interest.

"Well, that's about it," she concluded.

He nodded. "Consider your duty done. Now, tell me what's on your mind, and I promise not to interrupt this time. What's bothering you? Have you got a problem?"

"Well, the point is, I've only been at Geiger Associates a short while. You know I only arrived in New York a matter of weeks ago. I'll do all I can to help you, but there may be things you want to know that I can't answer."

Don waited, hands in pockets, observing her silently and seriously. After a brief pause, he said, "Is that it? That's the confession?" Then he relented. "Of course I know that, and I know you'll do your best, and I appreciate you giving up your valuable time. Now, what was the other thing?"

"I — I've got an apology to make. The

other day, at the Russian Tea Rooms."
She avoided meeting his eyes, choosing
instead to study his right ear lobe. "I
was in a bad mood, and I took it out
on you, accusing you of talking behind
my back. Selena soon put me right. I'm
sorry," she wound up.

"So you should be — I was going to
demand an apology if you hadn't got it
in first." Now she did meet his eyes,
and saw that he was joking. "Maybe we
were both a little hasty — or maybe the
summer heat's getting to us."

Ellen felt that a load had been removed
from her shoulders. It had been easy
after all, and everything was now clear
between them. And perhaps now he'd
begin to shed his over-protective attitude,
begin to see her as a woman to — the
phone rang and Don answered it.

"That was Mr. Geiger. He's ready to
see me now. Let's go."

Despite his initial casual attitude, Don
wasted no more time for the rest of the
day, starting with the meeting with the
Great Man, Geiger himself. She hadn't

met him before, had only seen him in the distance. Close up he wasn't as old as she thought, his greying hair still with sandy streaks, and he was tall and thin, wearing rimless glasses, his speech gentle and slow.

"Hi, Don, come on in," he said and then, when Ellen was introduced, amazed her by saying, "Hello Ellen, you're our English recruit, aren't you? I'm sorry not to have spoken with you before now, but with this merger it's Don I've been spending all my spare time with — we're regular buddies now. So how are you liking it here?"

"I love it," she assured him.

"Good. I expect you guys were all shocked when you heard about the new circumstances, but now you've met Don, you'll realise that it's a good thing. I know I'm happy about it. As far as I'm concerned, it was CZR or no one."

Don nodded. "We're honoured to be associated with the name of Geiger."

The two men exchanged a look that revealed to Ellen there was much left unsaid, then Mr. Geiger went on, "The advantages to us are enormous, and I'm sure when the dust's settled everyone will welcome the change here, don't you think so, Ellen?"

Ellen opened her mouth to speak, then hesitated. Would it be right to voice her — and others' — anxieties here? "I think what everyone would like to know is, why? I mean, the point about Geigers is that it was independent."

Ellen almost wished she hadn't asked her question, when she saw the look of weariness cross Mr. Geiger's face, but when he spoke his voice was strong.

"A good question, Ellen. The point is, there comes a time when going it alone makes no more sense. But I'm glad you mentioned it. I'll make a point of talking about that."

When they left Mr. Geiger's office, Don plunged her into a whirlwind of activity for the rest of the day, pulling her along in his wake rather than expecting her to lead the way. Although some of the time was spent chasing up files and facts and figures, much of it was spent in meeting and talking to people in other divisions. To Ellen's surprise Don appeared to enjoy this most of all, and was as happy chatting generally as about Geiger Associates' business. It didn't fit the picture of the man that Mark and Maggie had given her, but then Ellen had always felt uneasy with that media image of him.

During the day they had to pass through the stockbrokers' room several times. Don stopped to speak to a different person each time, and each time Ellen introduced him, and then stood back. And each time she received the same thinly veiled cold and resentful attitude, but she was so used to it that she hardly noticed it, and certainly didn't think that Don had.

At last, Don allowed his concentration to relax, and suggested they go back to his office and have some tea. They'd had lunch, of sorts; a sandwich brought in and eaten on the run.

"You do drink tea, don't you?" he asked. "Only my mother, the English half of me, never did. I only learned to love it later."

"Yes, thanks, you could stand a spoon up in my mum's brew!"

"OK, let's go over the day while we wait. I'd welcome your impressions."

"Oh — um — very successful, I think. You've covered everything very well in one day."

"Good." They were sitting down now, each in a leather armchair, and Don had taken his jacket and tie off, loosening his shirt at the neck. He suddenly appeared younger and, Ellen would have judged, more vulnerable if she hadn't been with him all day, seeing the expertise with which he dealt with both people and business.

"Ellen, you were telling Harold — Mr. Geiger — the truth there, when you said you were happy here? No problems settling in?"

Don's question took her off guard, and she quickly composed her features into a neutral expression. "Problems? No, none at all."

He eyed her speculatively, then said, "Sometimes an outsider, a foreigner, has a tough time being accepted. You haven't run into any of that?"

Ellen bit her lip, but answered his question steadily. "No, nothing like that."

"Only I could've sworn that back there, your colleagues, some of them anyway, were not too pleased to see you."

Ellen tried to brush his question aside. "Oh well, I've been here such a short while, I hardly know anybody." But she could tell Don wasn't deceived.

"OK, I understand you don't want to talk about it now — but when you do, I'll be ready to listen. Don't forget, will you?"

She read the concern in his eyes and was strongly tempted. Nothing would have been better than to let it all spill out, but she couldn't allow someone else to fight her battles for her. So she said, "Thanks," graciously this time, and quickly changed the subject. "What do

115

the initials CZR stand for?"

"It was originally Colleys Financial Management, then Colleys and Zebroski, and when I came along, we settled for CZR."

Without thinking, she said, "And now you'll have a G in there too, I suppose. Memorials in letters instead of scalps."

Don was quiet as their tea arrived, with bone china cups and a plate of cookies, but when they were alone again he said, "There's that resentment again. I felt it this morning, and then there were your comments when we were with Harold Geiger. It's not simply that you've been ordered on an assignment you don't want, is it? You resent the fact that CZR has merged with Geigers."

"I suppose I do," she answered reluctantly. "I mean, is merger just going to be a euphemism for takeover? Geigers is a respected old family firm, small enough for everyone to at least recognise everyone else. Now it'll be part of some giant conglomeration, swallowed up and soon forgotten. In the meantime, what about all the people whose lives will have been disrupted, who will've lost their jobs?"

"And what about all the people who will've benefited by it, have you thought of that? Nothing can stand still. If we all stayed in the same place, we'd slip backwards, like the Red Queen said in *'Alice'*. Life is about change and new challenges, otherwise it'd be hellish dull. I'm surprised at you trying to cling on to old patterns, Ellen. I thought you were all for trying out new adventures."

"Maybe, but should everything that's old be changed, just for the sake of it? Shouldn't the bits that work be left alone?"

"Of course, and who said Geigers was going to be turned upside-down? It doesn't have to happen that you and your friends will lose their jobs. You'll have to trust me when it comes to decision making time."

"Yes, I suppose so," Ellen conceded, and Don grinned unexpectedly.

"You make it sound as appetising as

posing beside a grizzly bear. How about if I promise you that nothing's going to happen overnight, will that make you feel better?"

"If anyone asks me, I'll tell them that's what you said," Ellen said sadly. She did trust him and yet — at the moment they seemed to be looking at one another across an unbridgeable chasm. It seemed they'd never agree on anything.

Don put down his teacup. "Don't worry, Ellen," he said more gently. "You'll get used to having me around."

"Oh no — I didn't mean to sound unwelcoming," Ellen said quickly. "You have to understand it's not — it's not personal." Why hadn't she realised that Don too would have feelings about this, just as sensitive as her own? "I mean, you made a very good impression on everyone you met today. They all liked you, I could tell."

"That's good, although I'll be happier when they respect me too."

"I'm sure they do. After all," she added, "everyone knows you're just about the best in your field. I can see now why you told me you have to live, breathe and eat figures."

Don stood up abruptly and prowled restlessly up and down the room. "I guess so, although I've been lucky to have a knack for this kind of thing. I don't know, sometimes I think, I don't know . . . " He broke off then flashed her another grin. "Hey, do you realise the time?" He pointed to the clock on the wall, which showed six-thirty. "I've an appointment this evening. I'm sorry, Ellen, but I'll have to leave you now."

Ellen felt obscurely disappointed. She felt that just then he'd been on the verge of telling her something, of revealing himself to her, but at the last moment he'd pulled back, hadn't allowed her a glimpse of what really made Don Redman tick. Was it some kind of survival instinct that made him keep all his secrets?

It felt strange to be away from him now. She'd been so aware of him all day, every nuance in his voice, every movement of his body, each expression on his face. Every now and then his hand would touch her arm to emphasise a point, or touch her waist as they moved along a corridor. From some men it would've annoyed her, but with Don — what was it? Was it impersonal, so that she couldn't take offence, or was it somehow part of a special bond between them, despite their differences? She didn't know — the only certainty was that she missed him already.

The brokers' room was almost empty. She stared disconsolately at her desk, began to shuffle through the pile of messages. There didn't appear to have been a crisis during her absence, she was glad to see. Then she came across a note from Maggie. *"Mark and I are In the Dice Box. Want to come and tell us all about it? Love Maggie."* Ellen smiled. Nothing would suit her better.

The Dice Box was a bar much frequented by the people from Geigers, and she'd been there several times after work. The dark green hood outside mounted on slender metal poles was decorated with large dice as well as announcing the name, but it was a long time since the days when it had been associated with gambling. She spotted Mark and Maggie straight away, waved, and went over.

"I feel as if I've been put through a wringer," she announced, placing her white linen jacket on the seat beside her.

"We got you a drink," Maggie said, jabbing her finger at a glass filled to the brim with a clear, colourless liquid and ice cubes. "A Manhattan. Think you can take it?"

"Anything, so long as it's cold." Ellen gulped at the ice-cold drink.

"Now tell us," Mark ordered. "Spill the beans. What have you been doing all day? I hope you were nice to your neighbour."

"You looked pretty pally when we saw you today," Maggie said. "So he didn't try to trip you up in any way?"

Ellen shook her head. "Don was great, he's so easy to get along with, and all the time he's storing everything away in that computer brain of his — and some of the questions! He just seemed to home in on Geigers' weak spots." She took another drink. "Unfortunately, I didn't do so well."

"Oh no!" Maggie exclaimed, while Mark groaned. "She blew it — I knew it!"

"Not as bad as that, but I did say I was worried about the merger, and he promised that nothing would happen straight away — and Mr. Geiger said he really didn't want to be independent any more, and you could tell that something was worrying him."

They all three looked at each other.

"I wonder if we can believe him?" Mark said thoughtfully, rubbing the condensation from the side of his glass of lager. "Don Redman's never been known to let the grass grow under his feet."

"And what about Mr. Geiger?" Maggie

asked. "What do you think was troubling him?"

But before Ellen could reply a voice behind her said, "Yes, Ellen, why not give us the benefit of your knowledge. For a newcomer, you sure haven't wasted any time. The question is, is he using you, or are you using him?"

It was Shirlee, and with her were Barry and Darryl with, in the background, Clyde.

"I don't know what you mean," Ellen said, puzzled.

"We knew something was up," Darryl said. "I mean, one day there's a guy doing his job, the next he's gone and there's someone all the way from England there — but we didn't realise quite how big it all was."

"And how exactly did Redman persuade Gieger to take you on as his spy?" put in Barry.

"Hey, lay off Ellen, will you?" Mark intervened, but Ellen put a restraining hand on his arm. This confrontation had been brewing since the day she'd arrived, she couldn't duck out of it now.

"I don't know what you're getting at," she said quietly. "I was already working for Geiger's London office when the job was advertised — but that was months ago, before Christmas, and I was told I had the job in January. I never met Mr. Redman till after I arrived, and then it was by accident. So now perhaps you'll tell me exactly what it is you're accusing me of doing?"

"You know, I really don't think she does know," Darryl said after a pause. "I mean, we can check her story now, and see if it fits."

"Of course she's telling the truth — so tell us now, what gives?" Mark demanded hotly, while Maggie nodded.

Shirlee spoke hesitantly. "You don't know about Hy? One Friday Abrams called him in, and when he came out he was white. Abrams was with him, wouldn't let him speak to anyone, and his desk was cleared in ten minutes and he was gone. No one's been able to track him down since. He was a good friend of ours — and then on Monday you arrived, and you were put at his desk."

"That's Abrams again," Maggie exclaimed. "He had it in for you before you arrived — he could've put you elsewhere, but he must've known how it would look to Hy's friends, when he was sacked like that."

Ellen gave a strangled laugh. "So at least I know it wasn't the shape of my nose that got to him."

"I remember Hy," Maggie said. "But I'd only just arrived, so I didn't know anything strange was going on."

Mark nodded. "He did leave kinda quick, but why think Ellen was connected?"

Darryl and Shirlee exchanged looks. "He was such a good friend, and we were so angry. No one would give us a straight answer. Abrams said family problems, but I don't believe he'd leave without telling us why."

"Well, I'm sorry," Ellen said, "but I can prove I was recruited months before any of this happened — which you could have found out if you'd asked me."

Shirlee sighed. "You're right. Apologies all round, I guess."

But although the other three seemed reluctantly satisfied, Ellen could tell from the look in Clyde's eyes that he still wasn't happy. And she was then quite sure that it had been his voice she'd heard that evening, spreading poison about her arrival.

5

"HELP yourself to more salad, there's plenty here," said Selena. Ellen's cousin had dropped round to her apartment late one evening with a takeaway Mexican meal and a miniature bottle of tequila for them to try, although Ellen had only taken a sip of the latter before deciding to stick with lemonade. However, she dipped into the spicy tacos with relish.

"This food is just right for a hot and humid New York night. I've only been able to tackle green salads during the day," Ellen said.

"It's too hot, isn't it — and this is only July. Wait until August — you'll feel like a wet dish rag."

"Great. You know, I miss not being able to open the windows — I know the double glazing keeps the air-conditioned air in, but I'd like to be able to look out at the night sky," Ellen said wistfully.

"Plus stopping you from being poisoned by the fumes, don't forget! Is that a note of homesickness there? Not having second thoughts about New York?"

"None," Ellen said firmly. "I'm practically a New Yorker now. I can even tell when different bits of your past are showing — sometimes you sound English, like your mum, sometimes Midwest, where you grew up — and sometimes you put on a deep south accent."

"Well, so ah do," Selena replied, exaggerating, then went on, "But I don't really like New York, not like you do — I mean, there's more to America than Manhattan, you know."

"You're right. Maybe I'll get a chance to explore, only I can't take a holiday yet. Just think, you could be sunning yourself in Florida right now, instead of — "

"Instead of having a boy friend who's crazy enough to want to spend the vacation working in New York!" Selena sighed, then reached up and loosened the chiffon bandana that kept her long, straight blonde hair from her face, and retied it more neatly. "But his parents insist. I guess I'm spoiled. Mom and Pop don't expect me to work. Anyway, I'm going to help out at a wine bar, save some money, and then we'll take off for a while before going back to college."

Ellen helped herself to another taco and salad. "You've got one more year to do, haven't you? What then?"

Selena shook her head. "Don't know. I wish I was like you, single-minded, ambitious. Say, how're things going with your new boss — it's weird thinking of you working with Don now."

Ellen laughed. "Not exactly with — and I've hardly seen him since that day I showed him around. But I know he's been very busy. Various bits of reorganisation going on. And he's got an assistant working with him. A beautiful woman with red hair. She was at your parents' party."

"I know who you mean. That's Cathy. Would it help if I told you she was happily married, with a little boy?" Selena said, giving Ellen a shrewd look. "Her husband's an artist, and he works at home and looks after the kid. They've got it all worked out."

Ellen had hoped her remark had sounded casual, indifferent, but Selena was too sharp for her. She tried to cover her tracks. "Oh, I don't think anyone's gossiped about the two of them. She seems really nice."

She failed. Selena grinned triumphantly. "I knew I was right — you've fallen for Don haven't you? The trouble is, he keeps his private life quite separate from his work — mainly to keep the newspaper reporters quiet — but I did hear his name connected with someone, only that was ages ago. Last year."

"Something's been troubling him. He nearly confided in me that day, and then didn't. You're right, he never gives anything away — except his opinions."

"I guess he's married to his work. That'll be the way to his heart, I guess. You'll have to get to him that way."

"Uh — uh." Ellen shook her head. "I know he's offered to help me — which I've refused — and I have had trouble at work, but — no. Don't you see? I've got to sort it all out myself."

"I think you're making a big mistake. You're being too stiff-necked about it. You'd better be careful, or you'll end up even more married to your job than he is — I mean independence is great, and all that, but it's nice to know someone loves you."

Ellen felt a stab at her heart. If only Selena knew how much she sometimes yearned for just that . . .

The atmosphere at Geigers was tense. Already the defections were beginning. One person made no secret of the fact that he was spending extended lunch hours with all his contacts, looking for a new job. Other firms, having heard the news about the merger, were already making huge offers to entice away the most talented of Geiger Associates' previously very loyal staff. Ellen could picture Mr. Harold Geiger at his desk, looking hurt and disappointed at this news. But what could he expect? Some people felt that he'd let them down, hadn't even given them any warning — and even more, no satisfactory explanation.

Ellen scanned the financial newspapers and journals carefully to see if any answers to the unexpected merger would turn up. But neither Don nor Geiger were giving interviews, and so the journalists had to be content with speculating wildly. Most of the sensible ones simply concluded that Geiger had decided, in today's economic climate of bigger and bigger companies, that he could no longer afford to stay on his own. Only one article disagreed, suggesting that Geiger Associates had not been making so much money as usual.

"What do you think, Maggie?" Ellen asked as they ate together in their favourite deli one lunchtime. "I suppose they're right — but I still don't agree that the company couldn't have stayed on its own."

"I guess Geiger no longer believed small was beautiful! But it's interesting that no one at all has even hinted that Don Redman might've pushed him into it."

"True. But why keep it a secret, and then spring it on us at the last moment?"

"I don't know. I expect we'll be told soon enough." Maggie paused, straightened her knife and fork on her plate. "Look, Ellen, we're all getting used to the idea now, and we've decided what we're going to do. I'm going to stay put; I don't know about — "

"Me too."

"Good. But it seems like you can't accept the change. Why's that?"

Ellen moved on her stool uncomfortably. "I'm not sure. I guess you're right, it's something to do with independence maybe . . . oh, I think I'll change the subject! I hear Mark's invited you for Sunday lunch, as well as me."

Maggie laid a hand on her arm. "OK, we'll change the subject — but think

133

about it. And yes, it'll be really great for us to put our feet up and let the man do all the cooking for a change. You know, I really feel I've been getting into a rut lately. It's good to do something different at the weekend."

"I know — reading the papers, making notes, doing the washing." Ellen was pleased to hear that Maggie was looking forward to their Sunday out. She'd been getting over a broken engagement for some months, and she hadn't shown any interest in going out with another man. Ellen, foolishly perhaps she knew, secretly hoped that Maggie might succumb to Mark's handsome charm. "Let's just hope things don't hot up this weekend and we have to come into the office, or attend a meeting — I mean, I love my job, but it would be great to have an uninterrupted break for once."

"Too true."

Suddenly, sitting there on her high stool, hearing the American voices loud and easy around her, feeling the heat sweep in through the open door in waves, and seeing the traffic outside, bumper to bumper, the yellow cabs, the sidewalks packed with people, Ellen felt a strange burst of exhilaration.

OK, so Geigers was going to merge. OK, so Don Redman hadn't spoken to her, sought her out, for over a week. But she was still here. Nothing had shaken her sense of purpose, not even Abrams' enmity. Two months, and she could at last feel established, begin really to enjoy being with the new people and new family she'd met.

It was as if there'd been a time lag on her happiness, a jet lag which had suddenly lifted, so that she only now felt, truly, that she'd arrived, despite the problems that hovered on the edge of her life. She smiled happily at Maggie, squeezed her arm, and said, "Maybe life isn't so bad after all?"

Maggie gave her an answering smile. "No, not too bad at all."

Early the following week, feeling more limp and drained than ever by the rising, oppressive heat which was making everyone short-tempered, Ellen was at her monitor, following some strange things that were happening to the price of wheat. She'd read that devastating storms had been forecast for the Midwest, and if the weathermen were right this once the harvests might be spoiled. Some people, however, thought it was cleverer to believe that the weathermen were quite wrong, and they wanted to buy wheat shares. Ellen was trying to make up her mind which was the right course of action to follow. She felt like playing safe, but was she right? Should she follow her instinct, or . . .

She became aware of a slight stir, a subtle change in the atmosphere of the room, and when she saw Don she knew it was because of him. Her heart performed several cartwheels, and her mind went a blank, but she kept her fingers steady. He seemed to be making towards her, and her scalp tingled with anticipation. And then Don was standing beside her, one hand thrust casually in his trouser pocket, the other leaning on her desk. The figures in front of her now looked meaningless, the pattern they normally made for her was gone.

"How goes it?" he enquired.

"Fine," she managed.

"Wheat market prices, yes? Have you decided what you're going to do?"

"Yes. I'm — I'm going to sell."

Instantly her mind whirled. She hadn't been contemplating selling at all, but somehow she felt she had to appear decisive in front of him, otherwise he'd be sure to try to offer some help. She tried to read his expression covertly from the corner of her eye, but he wasn't giving anything away. He looked mildly interested as she spoke into the phone, and punched figures into the computer.

"I'm only selling in the Illinois Corporation," she told him, fingers mentally crossed that she'd made the right decision.

"Sounds good to me." He straightened up, and Ellen felt an easing of the tension his presence always induced in her. "Ellen, I'm sorry I've not been around lately, but I've been very busy — and now things are easing off will you have dinner with me? Tonight?"

"Tonight? Um, I'd love to, but — " How could she accuse Don ever of letting his work come before everything else? She had meetings that evening, and an appointment the following evening too.

"You're a busy lady," he said, reading her diary over her shoulder. "Here, let me write myself in for the day after tomorrow — before it's too late."

Ellen breathed a sigh of relief. He wasn't going to be put off. Her heart sang, she couldn't keep the smile from her face as she looked up at him — that is, until the moment when he said, "I've never thanked you properly for showing me around the other day, so I hope this will show you how much I appreciated it."

Ellen's phone ringing interrupted, to her disappointment. As she answered it Don touched her shoulder briefly, then walked away. She watched his disappearing back as she listened to Mr. Renkovic's nasal tones. "Did you give my suggestion any further thought?" he asked.

"About metals? Yes, Mr. Renkovic, I've kept an open mind, but I haven't seen any reason why I should buy for you."

"It's a feeling I got. I think you should."

"Well, it's really slack at the moment. No one seems interested, and I haven't heard any rumours."

"Yeah, I suppose you're right. But keep an eye on them for me, will ya?" Ellen promised, and as she replaced the receiver she was thankful that Mr. Renkovic had been so compliant. She had expected him to argue with her, after everything she'd heard about him. Could there be something in what he said? It was a wild idea, but she'd keep her promise. She smiled as she realised that she rather liked him.

Ellen was still floating with happiness at the prospect of dinner with Don, whatever the reason, when her direct desk intercom with Abrams buzzed.

"Huntsworth — I want you in here, now."

Her heart plummeted. She no longer feared him, but she couldn't help feeling dread. What was he going to fling at her now?

As soon as she entered the outer office he saw her, through the open communicating door, and his enraged bellow caught her off guard. She exchanged glances with a sympathetic Karen.

"Huntsworth — what the hell are you doing out there, doodling? I want an explanation for this." And he shook some papers at her. She went towards him saying, "I'll explain them if I can. Perhaps you can show me . . . " and her voice, miraculously, was not trembling. But this only seemed to enrage him more, and he mimicked her English accent mockingly.

"Oh do come and explain. I'll be *so* happy to hear!" and he tossed the papers on to his desk without looking, so that some fell on the floor.

Seething, Ellen was glad to be inside his office with the door shut while she bent to pick up the papers, as he expected. The whole brokers' floor would've been able to hear his raised voice. At the same time she had a horrible feeling that perhaps, this once, he was right to accuse her — in which case, would Don get to hear about it?

"Look here," he took a piece of paper from her grasp and jabbed at it with a stubby finger. "The Commission's been on to the firm, and we've traced this code number to your computer. Now this here deal was made two months ago, and there's been no confirmation, nothing."

Mixed anger and anxiety seeping coldly through her veins and she took the sheet and studied it. It was certainly her code number, yet it looked unfamiliar.

"I'll need to consult my files, then I'll sort this out."

"You're not running out on me so

easily. Next thing I know you'll be going to your friend Redman for protection, to cover up for your mistakes. I want an explanation right now — and yes, you can drop the shocked look, I know all about you and Redman. You thought you covered up for it the other day."

"Mr. Redman is not my 'friend'!"

"Oh yeah? Well, I heard otherwise, and I believe it. The question is, just how far does your pillow talk go, eh?" He sneered. "Is it tips from the top, or do you whisper juicy pieces of office gossip into his ear? Not that I care, and you can tell him that from me. I told Geiger we didn't need any Britishers in this office."

"How dare you! I was telling you the truth just now, though it's none of your business what I do out of office hours. But to imply that I betray confidences — that I — and — " Ellen ran out of words as her indignation got the better of her. She looked down at the paper she'd taken back from Abrams for inspiration, and immediately grasped the answer to it all. "And if you'll look right here, you'll see this sheet is dated five days before I started working here — so it must've been my predecessor's deal, not mine. Same computer code, but you'd have known if you hadn't been so ready to try to find fault with me."

Leaving Abrams standing stunned in the middle of his office, she marched out, managing to restrain herself from closing the door too loudly behind her.

She was still fuming hours later, outraged by Abrams' attitude and the way he had it in for her. It seemed as if he'd formed some sort of prejudice about her before she'd even arrived — perhaps he didn't like English people, or perhaps he didn't like the way Mr. Geiger had taken her on. But he had no excuse for behaving the way he did. Ellen knew she could go to Mr. Geiger — or even to Don — and make a complaint, but she didn't want to do that. It would feel like telling tales, and it would certainly look as if she couldn't fight her own battles. It was then, when she least needed it, that strange things began to happen in the metal market. She had determined to leave earlier than her usual seven o'clock, having tied up all her business, and was giving a last glance at the closing prices for Mr. Renkovic's sake, when she saw that those particular figures had shown a sudden leap upwards.

Ellen stared at the screen, transfixed. Renkovic had been right after all! Something was happening out there, and she hadn't had an inkling of it coming. What was she to do? Renkovic was sure to find out — she was surprised he hadn't been on the phone already, telling her aggrievedly that she should have backed his judgment.

Resolutely she took off her light cotton jacket, dropped her handbag back into her bottom drawer, and drew the directory towards her. She'd have to go through Chicago and San Francisco now — and it looked like she wasn't going to be leaving for some time.

Talking non-stop, not even halting to

allow herself to think, Ellen worked feverishly over the next hour. And when it was all over she was sure Mr. Renkovic would be pleased. She had noticed what was going on in time, had invested plenty of his money. He was bound to make a killing.

Feeling quite drained Ellen made her way out into the warm evening air. She had to admit that the crisis had been exciting, and she was pleased that she'd been able to react so quickly and get on top of the situation. That was, after all, what her job was all about. 'So, Don Redman,' she thought, 'what do you make of that? My first real crisis, and I came through. Nothing to it. No need to warn me about being eaten alive by the sharks out there. Whether they're impersonal or come in the shape of Abrams, I can cope.'

Her feeling of triumph was short-lived. A few hours into trading the next day came news of a dramatic takeover, which would have been bad enough if it hadn't been followed immediately by a tragic mining disaster, and the metal prices dropped disastrously. Ellen's horror of yesterday evening was nothing compared with the feeling with which she contemplated the dancing electronic figures in front of her. She'd been tricked, caught out — OK, so plenty of others must have been too — as well as simply unlucky. Now Mr. Renkovic stood to lose a lot of money instead of gain a profit.

Ellen closed her eyes in momentary despair. If only she'd stuck to her original decision. Perhaps she'd over-reacted because she'd been so upset by her confrontation by Abrams who, thank goodness, was keeping well out of sight today. But that was no good either, blaming someone else for her mistakes.

The phone rang and she knew, before picking it up, that it would be Mr. Renkovic. To her surprise he sounded sheepish. "You were so right, Miss Huntsworth, and I'm real glad you advised against me."

She had to own up. "As a matter

of fact I did buy in, but not with everything you had, and at an early price. It could've been a lot worse, and I'll do what I can."

"That's OK," he said sadly when she'd explained what had happened. "I was at a baseball game last night — my nephew was playing — but if I'd been in I might've asked you to risk everything. But you're the first person to take my intuition seriously — and look what a fine mess it's got us in."

Ellen wrestled for the rest of that morning with the problem of how to salvage what she could. She was sure that there must be some clever way out if only she could think of it. She could always talk it over with some of the other brokers. Immediately she knew that Don was the one person who'd have exactly the right answer to the problem. She clenched her fists. No, she couldn't, she wouldn't, go to him. She'd told him right at the start, and she wasn't going back on her word now.

But was it right to put her own

personal feelings before the good of her clients? By talking it over with Don she might save all of Mr. Renkovic's money. All she had to do was buzz through to his personal assistant, Cathy, on the intercom, and ask for an interview. Of course, it was having an unfair advantage, she knew that, to feel confident that he would be prepared to see her right away. But then wasn't it right to talk to a senior person who could advise her? Her hand reached out, hesitated.

No, there had to be some other way. She couldn't climb down now. Maybe when it was all over, when they had dinner, she could ask him — without telling him the details — what he would have done in her situation. Then she could learn from the experience. And if things got worse, she'd call him in anyway. Talking to Abrams was, of course, out of the question.

Ellen scarcely lifted her eyes from the monitors, except to call out to other brokers across the room figures and questions. Maggie, realising that something was up, tactfully brought her a sandwich and a cold drink so that she wouldn't even have to go out for lunch. Mark tried to talk to her, but gave up when he received only vague grunts.

At last, at last, through a complicated manoeuvre, Ellen thought she'd found a solution. She was also relieved to see that, because she hadn't panicked but had waited, that the prices had stopped falling and were stabilising. She discovered that she'd been so tense that her stomach was tied in knots and her head was throbbing. More than that, though, was the relief that she'd be able to discuss it with Don, tomorrow, as a hypothetical problem.

Dinner with Don. It was still a dream. She couldn't dare hope that it would actually happen, and half expected a call to say that business had got in the way and he'd have to cancel. There was still time for that to happen, right up until the last moment. At least with all the worry of the last few days she felt she'd lost several pounds in weight, and that would ensure that she'd be able to fit comfortably into a particularly stunning dress she'd seen, and which she was determined to buy, even though it meant budgeting severely till the end of the month.

Would she be able to hide her feelings for Don, sitting across some candlelit table from him? Surely he'd be able to tell, without the distractions of other people and work, the devotion in her eyes? Her heart continued to sing as she waited for their evening together.

The restaurant Don took her to was in the quiet Gramercy Park area, and it was an Italian place, busy and lively, with excellent food. There were red checked tablecloths on solid wood tables, a spray of fresh flowers in a vase on each table, and the cheerful waiters called out to one another in Italian. They ate a tasty spaghetti *vongole,* with tiny clams and mussels, and Ellen then had chicken, while Don tackled a more exotic steak tartare, and for dessert, neither of them could resist the fresh profiteroles, doused in hot chocolate sauce.

It was very far from the intimate, candlelit scene Ellen had fantasised about. In this jolly place it was easy to talk in a relaxed, friendly way. Don didn't once question her about the advisability of her staying in New York, and when the subject came up, he deliberately steered the conversation away from Geiger Associates. Ellen was relieved of worrying about whether she would be tempted to ask for advice, or to give way to her feelings about Abrams.

While they talked about films and music, exchanged jokes and stories, when it came to his personal life, Ellen found herself politely but firmly blocked. She gathered his parents had both died some years before, that he had a sister and plenty of aunts, uncles, cousins and even grandparents. But that was it. She found, instead, that he listened attentively when she described her own family and life in England. She was left completely frustrated about what he did in the evenings and, more importantly, who with.

Ellen did feel, however, a returning flare of hope. He had invited her out and she imagined she saw, although quickly veiled, a flicker in his eyes that resembled the one when they'd met at her aunt and uncle's party. It was peculiar, she thought. Men were supposed to find women difficult to understand, but she was having a hard time trying to penetrate Don's urbane, sophisticated exterior. She felt he was attracted to her and yet . . .

Don paid for their meal, and they took a taxi back to their apartment building, the windows wound down to catch some breeze. The odours and sounds of the city, as alive now near midnight as it was at midday, came in to them. Bright lights and neon signs flashed, the sidewalks buzzed with people.

Joe greeted them as they crossed the foyer, and Ellen wasn't sure, but she thought he gave her the ghost of a wink.

Inside the elevator Ellen said, "Thanks for a lovely evening. I really enjoyed it, though it wasn't really necessary to make up for the other day. I enjoyed that too."

"I know — I enjoyed it too. But I feel — responsible for you."

The smile left Ellen's face. That was the last thing she wanted to hear. Had he invited her out simply because of that misplaced sense of duty of his? Keeping an eye on her was another way of putting it. If he only realised, the last thing she wanted was to be protected. Instead, she longed for him to sweep her dangerously off her feet, flinging caution to the winds. His voice brought her back to earth.

"I'll see you to your door," he was saying, and she realised that they'd reached her floor.

"Oh thanks," Ellen said, wondering if she should point out to him that she had safely made her way back to her apartment alone at night on numerous occasions. But she decided she didn't want to spoil the delightful evening at that late stage. However, she felt flustered at having him stand so near and, fumbling for her keys, clumsily dropped them.

"Here, I'll get them — "

"No, it's perfectly all right I — "

They both stooped and then, straightening up, collided with one another.

"Are you all right?" Don steadied her, his arm around her, and she looked up at him, and then his arms were tightening around her. A spark seemed to leap between them, his clear grey eyes darkened, and then she closed her eyes as his lips met hers.

Somewhere, in a dream, their lips melted together, and then he traced a pattern of kisses across her cheek and then her neck. Ellen put her arms around him, her fingers entwined in his hair. She could smell the fresh tang of him, feel his heart thudding powerfully against her.

It felt so right to be in his arms. No other kiss had felt like this, and Ellen never wanted it to stop. To be in his arms — it was a dream come true. Then, suddenly, he was drawing away from her.

"Ellen, this is all wrong. I'm sorry," he said, his voice low.

"Sorry?" she repeated stupidly, aware that her voice was not quite steady.

"Yes — how's it going to look? That I'm your boss, wining and dining you before asking for favours? Fattening you up for the kill?"

"That never occurred to me," Ellen declared. "Besides, who will know?"

"I know — and I refuse to take advantage of you. The fact that you're new in town, don't know your way around — " He stopped, took a step away from her, and she could see his composure returning, like a shield between them, that infuriating, charming smile that hid his emotions appearing on his lips. "A goodnight kiss, Ellen, that's all it was."

"The new girl in town, huh? Doesn't know what to do when a man kisses her — is that what you believe? Well let me tell you — " Ellen, stung into defending herself, was stayed by Don's hand on her arm.

"Believe me, you'll be grateful in the morning. Tonight we've been — close, friends. Tomorrow, though, you'll see that it's better not to become involved with me."

"Tomorrow I'll be grateful — don't you ever lose control? Don't you ever let that mask slip and tell someone, anyone, just what's going on inside?"

Don's mouth and his grip on her arm tightened. "Let the mask slip — and couldn't I accuse you of the same? I know those other stockbrokers are freezing you out, I know you must be experiencing at least one problem at work, but will you tell me about it? No. You're the one who won't unbend an inch."

"That was a misunderstanding. I dealt with it myself and it's all cleared up now. But how did you — ?"

"I could tell, it was obvious to anyone what was going on." He released her. "You're just too damn proud to ask for help. Your lips may be yielding, but inside you're busy building a defensive wall."

Ellen took a deep breath, wanting to match his cool composure. "I've been trying to tell you all along, I appreciate your concern but it's really unnecessary. You were telling me about taking risks the other day, and you're right. My feelings about Geiger Associates were only sentimentality. I do prefer adventure."

He smiled slightly. "I understand what you're trying to tell me — but I promise you, being more than my friend would bring you far more than you'd ever bargained for. Not adventure, but foolhardy, head-on collision with danger. And now good night, Ellen, before we say anything more we're likely to regret." And with that he reached out, touched her hair lightly, and turned to leave.

Once indoors Ellen touched her mouth with fingers that still shook a little from emotion, then snatched them away. What was going on? She knew she should feel ashamed — she'd practically thrown herself at Don there, and he hadn't been able to hide that he'd enjoyed kissing her. Now he was trying to frighten her off, and had slunk away almost as if he'd been guilty of something. Ellen shook her head. Whatever it was, the last person he was going to tell was her.

6

THE July days slipped by so fast that Ellen found she barely had time to fit everything in. Despite the fact that it was high summer, and people everywhere in the Northern hemisphere were either sitting on, or dreaming about, or planning to sit on, golden beaches, the stock market didn't let up its relentless pace. It was winter in the southern hemisphere, and someone, somewhere, whatever the weather, was wanting to buy or sell. The market was perhaps quieter than in the spring, but it still felt busier to Ellen than London.

She found that, instead of jumping out of bed in the morning, she was rolling out, bleary eyed, and was sometimes halfway to the subway before she really knew that she wasn't asleep any longer. By eleven a.m. she was feeling limp and distracted, and by four in the afternoon she was finding it hard to keep herself from snapping at people; everyone was suffering from an edgy irritation. In the evenings, if she wasn't at a meeting, or out with Maggie, Mark or Selena, she sat up late with books and papers, endlessly fascinated by the figures in front of her, until they blurred and she dragged herself to bed to fall into a deep and dreamless sleep.

The Renkovic crisis had passed, and Ellen had salvaged something from the wreckage. And, although there had already been a change of faces in the stockbroking office, the atmosphere had begun to calm down in the absence of any immediate announcements about changes at Geigers.

It was by losing herself in ceaseless activity that Ellen hoped to forget those dizzying, delirious moments when she'd been in Don's arms and his lips had imprinted themselves on hers — she was sure she could never contemplate any other man kissing her now.

He'd apologised, he'd made a mistake, he'd said. Yet in those few moments she'd felt sure they were as one, so when he'd drawn away from her afterwards . . . But maybe she'd been wrong, imagined it? After all, what did it matter anyway?

Don Redman had long ago decided her place in his life; he was determined to keep her filed away under 'untouchable'. She was the nice young girl to be saved from danger, and there was no way in which she could be considered as in the running for his heart. She wasn't even a contender, and she thought she knew the sort of woman who would be — tall, with long legs, a jet set model, perhaps, more at home in the South of France or Barbados that in a home. But Ellen knew she was being unfair to her long-legged rival — she was simply jealous, and where Don was concerned, her normal reasoning flew out of the window.

Not knowing how he spent the rest of his life made her jealousy worse. Could she be sure that there was nothing between him and his assistant, Cathy? Somehow she thought that if she knew it wouldn't be so bad. He'd been careful, though, to give nothing away while they dined. Not a name, nor even a casual reference to 'we', had crossed his lips. The only women he'd mentioned had been members of his family. Admittedly, Ellen hadn't gone out of her way to refer to past boy friends, either.

She was glad to accept when, one Thursday afternoon, Mark asked her if she would go with him to see a new film. "It's supposed to be terrible," he'd said, "but I like the stars. Want to give it a try?"

She'd nodded. Anything was worth trying to keep Don Redman from centre stage of her thoughts. Then, later on, riding down in the elevator after work, Maggie had asked, rather diffidently of her, "What're you doing on Saturday night? Can you come to a party with me then? You can come over for a meal first." She'd paused, then added, "Ross is going to be there." Ross was her ex-fiance.

"I'd love to — I'd arranged something

162

else, but I'm sure I can rearrange it easily. I'll call you later."

Maggie flashed her quick brilliant smile. "If you're willing to do that, it can't be with Mr. Redman."

Ellen had told her about their dinner together, but no one else — there was no point in fanning the flames of gossip. "No," she said sadly. "Mark suggested we go see a film together, but it's not that good."

"Oh." Maggie had looked away quickly, but not before Ellen had caught a glimpse of something in her eyes. Disappointment?

"I promise you, he wasn't that keen. It was just something to do. I think he'd much rather go to the party."

"OK. That'd be nice. Ask him, anyway — he'll be very welcome."

Ellen worried about Maggie's reaction as she made her way home. As a threesome she and Maggie and Mark got on well together. Maggie's sharp wit contrasted with Mark's good-natured sense of fun. But three was a difficult number, you could never be sure if one wasn't feeling a bit left out. Perhaps Maggie felt that Mark was an intruder on their original friendship.

So Ross was going to be at the party. Ellen could see why it would be hard for Maggie. They'd split up at Christmas after a two-year engagement. They'd both decided that they weren't right for each other, but even so, they'd been close for a long time, and Maggie had been slow to recover. Ellen knew that Maggie was beginning to build a new life for herself especially through someone like Ellen, who'd never known her and Ross as a couple. Now she'd be seeing him again for the first time in months, among old friends, and perhaps he'd have a new girl friend. It had to be done — she wouldn't want to avoid her old friends.

But Ellen also wondered, could the closeness she'd sensed growing between Maggie and Mark have something to do with that look of disappointment? It was just like Mark's open nature not to consider that asking Ellen to see the film might hurt Maggie. She sighed.

Triangles — they just didn't work.

She'd just replaced the receiver at home after speaking to Mark, who had jumped at the chance of going to the party, when it rang again beneath her hand. As always, her heart thudded for a moment, hoping to hear Don's voice, but it was Selena. She sounded very excited, and launched into a breathless torrent of words, finishing up with, "Isn't that just great? Can't you wait to feel the sea around your legs?"

"What's this? Slow down," Ellen laughed. "Did you say something about a vineyard? Where's that?"

"That's where, idiot. Martha's Vineyard, an island on the coast, and it's beautiful. The sea is fantastic, and we'll have the whole weekend just to relax and wash the city out of our hair. Do say you'll come!"

"I'd love to — but won't Sammy mind me tagging along?"

"Of course not. We've got to have someone to keep his parents occupied! They rented this place on the spur of the moment — fed up with the city — a few days ago, and they've gone up already. They're great and they love having lots of people about, plus they're dying to meet you. We'll leave as early as you can get away on Friday, and we can go by bus — Sammy's taking his bike up but I'll ride with you, if you can come. Say you will."

"That's too tempting." Ellen thought quickly. There was no reason why she couldn't come in late on Monday morning — Abrams surely wouldn't refuse her that. And if she was lucky she could get away at six on the Friday. As for Maggie's party — it was just the excuse she needed to get Maggie and Mark on their own together and see what happened. "If you're sure it's OK with Sammy's parents — I'll be there!"

The traffic crawled nose to tail out of Manhattan, speeding up a little once out on the freeway, but still too crowded to go at any real speed. Ellen and Selena sat in air-conditioned comfort, watching the smooth, wooded landscape slip by once they left the suburbs behind, beyond the glare-proof windows of the bus. They were both dressed in holiday clothes, Selena in tight lime green cotton pants and a white baggy T-shirt with a slogan emblazoned across the front, bare feet thrust into sandals, her hair braided away from her petal pink and soft white complexion. Ellen wore a matching shirt and skirt in a bold bright pattern, and she'd tied her hair back in a ponytail. Both were in holiday mood, and talked most of the journey away.

"Can you stay over till Monday?" Selena asked.

"Yup," Ellen nodded. "I thought I'd have a fight on my hands with Abrams, but he signed my request form. Perhaps he's planning to replace me before I get back some time Monday morning!"

"I hope not — but that's great. I'm only part time at the wine bar, so I can stay as long as I want. I can't wait to get to the beach — and to be with Sammy out there — so romantic. One more weekend in the city and I'd've died."

"Me too," Ellen said with such feeling that Selena turned to look at her.

"Wow — is that Abrams really getting to you? You've played it down, but I'm wondering if you should complain to someone."

Ellen shook her head. "It's not just Abrams — it's everything. I just need a break." Especially from being in love with Don Redman, she added silently.

It was twilight by the time they reached their destination, the last part by taxi over uneven roads. Amid tall, leafy trees were dotted large rambling clapboard houses, each with a veranda and wide, open grounds. Here and there a globe lamp glowed, throwing a halo of light on to leaves stirring in the breeze from the sea, sending dark patterns swirling across the rough track. As they walked up to the house they could hear the faint swish of the sea, and the hoot of an owl.

Selena was greeted with an enthusiastic hug from Sammy, who'd heard their taxi.

Tall, open-faced, he was wearing cotton khaki shirt and trousers. Ellen liked him very much.

"Come and meet Mom and Pop," he said, letting them in through the front door. "They're out back. I'll carry your bags," and he swung them effortlessly over one shoulder and followed them through.

On the back veranda were comfortable cane chairs, and lights hung here and there in trees revealed an expanse of grass, trees and shrubland beyond. Around the porchlight was a great cloud of moths and insects. Here the sound of the sea was much stronger.

"Hello. Glad you could make it." Lee and Honor, Sammy's father and mother, immediately made Ellen feel at home. "We're planning a barbecue, been waiting for you to arrive."

"Hope you like your food black on the outside, red inside!"

"OK, Sammy," Honor said. "For that you can go and check the charcoal."

"Only kidding, Mom. Only I'm

starving, and I bet Selena and Ellen are too."

"Using the girls as an excuse to get started, huh?" said a voice from the doorway. There was a moment's silence, then Selena's delighted squeal. "Don, what are you doing here?" as she launched herself at him and hugged him enthusiastically. To Ellen's ears it sounded like genuine surprise, but she'd tackle her cousin about it later anyway, she thought grimly.

"We were just waiting for our other guest," Lee was explaining. "Don's been having a shower — and I think you know each other, don't you?"

"Yes, we do," Ellen said. Don looked quite different tonight. He was wearing a loose white shirt over faded blue jeans, his hair still damp from the shower. He took her hand momentarily and smiled down at her, and all her disappointment and frustration vanished as if they'd never been.

"How are you?" Don was asking, but before she could reply Sammy had grabbed Don by the arm.

"At last!" he said. "Now I can get something to eat — come and help me."

While the food was prepared, everyone lent a hand, and the conversation was light and bantering. Ellen floated through it all, conscious only of Don's voice and glance. Then, plates heaped high with freshly made hamburgers, sausages, steaks and salad, Lee and Honor retired to the veranda, while Sammy and Selena sat on the grass near the barbecue. "He doesn't want to get too far away from a second helping," Selena explained.

Don took her elbow. "Let's sit on the veranda steps," he suggested, "and I'll get us some wine."

Ellen stared at her plate, her earlier appetite severely impaired. Don was here for the weekend. Far from getting away from him, they were going to be thrown together at every opportunity. Her mind reeled at the thought, and when he returned with the wine she sipped it carefully.

"It'll be a bit quiet for you here, far away from the city," he said. "No bright lights."

"You may miss them, but it sounds wonderful to me," she contradicted. "It's heaven to hear nothing but the rustling of leaves, and the sea in the distance." She was silent for a moment, then said, "I hope this doesn't upset your plans, cause any inconvenience, me being here this weekend. I didn't know that you — "

"As long as you're willing to forget that Wall Street and the stock market even exist, I think we'll get along fine, because my only plans are for swimming and lazing in the sun and relaxing completely." He grinned. "Or are you planning something much more energetic?"

"What you've just described sounds idyllic. It's enchanting here, isn't it?"

"When Lee and Honor got the chance to take this place they were right not to let it slip by. Lee's running his own company now, small, but his time's his own."

"Was it Sammy who invited you

here?" she asked quickly.

"Uh — uh. I've known Lee from way back. We worked together in — "

"Uh-*uh,*" Ellen wagged a finger at him. "You nearly broke your own rule. We've left that world of work far behind."

"That's right, you tell him Ellen," Sammy said, passing by to fetch some wine.

"In fact it was Lee who suggested me to your aunt and uncle — so we have Selena and Sammy to thank for the connection," but even as he spoke Don was laying his plate aside. "What's that — there, did you see?" He gripped her wrist. "C'mon, I think I know what it is." And he led her across the rough grass towards the trees and bushes. "We need to be away those lights," he said.

Soon they were in semi-darkness, in a small grove of tall trees, leaves whispering lightly. Don stopped and stationed her in front of him. "The trick is not to look directly into the darkness, but try to see what's on the edge of your vision, after your eyes have adjusted."

"I don't understand what — oh yes, there it is," Ellen cried delightedly.

"I thought so — fireflies," Don told her.

The softly flashing lights of the fireflies, an eerie, almost greenish light, floated in the darkness. "How beautiful," Ellen said softly. "I've never seen them before."

Unconsciously, Don's arm had slipped around her waist. "I always used to look for fireflies when I was a boy. I tried to catch them, but if you did, the little lights went out so soon. Such ephemeral creatures. How sad it is they only live for such a short time."

Ellen could feel the steady beat of his heart through their thin clothing, could feel the heat from his body, the easy grasp of his arm around her. His face was a pale blur in the night. Suddenly she felt that, if she'd been destined to live a life as ephemeral as the firefly, she'd have chosen to spend it all in this moment, close to Don. As if reading her thoughts, she felt his arm tighten, and she began to turn towards him, their breathing the only sound above the hiss of the sea along the shore. Then a call from the direction of the house broke the spell between them.

"Hey Don, Ellen, c'mon and help yourself to pork chops." It was Lee. They exchanged smiles.

"Don, the food is fantastic, but I don't think I can eat any more."

"What, giving up on the American diet already? Don't worry, I'll eat yours — but you'll regret it tomorrow when we go swimming."

Don's deliberate cheerfulness couldn't hide from them both the feeling of closeness which had sprung into being and, despite the abrupt interruption, it had not been broken. As they sat with the others and talked and laughed the rest of the evening away, she felt when his gaze rested on her it was somehow special, and she sat in a kind of aura of happiness. Selena caught her eye and winked, and Ellen looked at her suspiciously. Had Selena known that

175

Don would be here?

She didn't have to look at Don to know that he was there, and she felt she could drift away on that cloud of happiness. That night she fell asleep as soon as her head made contact with the pillow, and when she at last awoke it was past nine o'clock, the sun was streaming through the sprigged cotton curtains.

It was impossible to remember any other way of life but this. Down on the sun-bleached boards of the back veranda Ellen breakfasted with Selena, drinking coffee and orange juice, and eating home-baked American muffins with butter and jam. In the deep blue sky was a speckle of small white clouds being driven inland by the steady sea breeze. She could smell the tang of salt in the air, and the sun was hot on her bare feet.

"Everyone else has gone to the beach," Selena said. "I told them not to wait for us. Want to swim and sunbathe this morning?"

"Can't think of anything I'd like

better." Ellen selected another muffin, split it open, then fixed Selena with an accusing glare. "I guess you didn't know Don was going to be here?"

"I swear it — but even if I had, I don't think I'd've told you. What a perfect way to get the two of you together."

Ellen couldn't help grinning. "I have to admit, it was a lovely surprise. You know, it was like meeting him all over again for the first time, but without the prickly bits."

"Well, you've got me and Sammy to thank for bringing us all together."

"I know — and don't worry, I'll keep a level head."

Selena regarded her seriously. "You do that. Don's a great guy, but I bet you he's broken a few hearts in his time."

After they'd finished they washed up and tidied the kitchen, then put bikinis under protective shirts and strolled across the garden towards the beach. Selena's bikini was orange spotted with black, Ellen's a sea jade which contrasted with the red glints in her hair. Her creamy skin had a faint dusting of freckles across the shoulders due to those auburn tints, but with careful use of suntan creams she was able to take the sun.

Even though she wore a perfectly standard bikini, as they neared the beach she began to feel uneasy. She could guess that Don would have a good physique from the way he moved, but she felt shy at the thought of his eyes on her.

The grounds gave way to sand dunes covered in tough grass, and then they were over the other side, the stiff breeze whipping at their hair, walking across fine silver sand, the sea rolling with a boom and a hiss only a few yards away. Honor and Lee had erected windbreaks and were sunbathing on comfortable loungers.

"You've missed the boys," Lee said. "There were having a race to that rocky point over there."

"Oh yes, I see them, one blond head and one dark. I think Don's slightly ahead, so I'd better go and cheer Sammy on. Coming?" But before Ellen could reply Selena had tossed off her shirt and was running across the firm sand to dive into the water.

Honor smiled and shook her head. "Such energy," she murmured, while Lee agreed. "She and Sammy make a good match," then she said, "Are you joining us here, Ellen? We've already had our swim."

"Thanks, I think I'll go in now," she decided. "See you later."

She crossed the sand to the waves, then ran in. The water was stingingly cold, but as she flung herself into it her swimming soon warmed her up. She ducked under the waves, resurfaced and then, in the foamy breakers, lost sight of her cousin and the two men. She struck out in their direction in a crawl but soon found herself running out of breath. She'd neglected her physical fitness, she realised, switching to a steady breaststroke.

She should have reached the others

by now, and began to feel anxious that she'd missed them. She seemed to have been swimming for some time. She tried to lift her head high, but the big waves obscured her vision. She saw instead that she was near the rocks of the point. She decided to head for the shore.

It wasn't as easy as she thought. There seemed to be a strong undertow here and she found she was making little headway. Then she heard Don's voice above the sound of the sea.

"Ellen — everything OK?"

"There's — some — kind of — current," she called back.

"OK. Swim towards me."

Feeling the strength fading from her muscles Ellen called back. "Can't — see you," trying to keep the panic from her voice.

"Stay where you are." It was all she could do to keep herself from being buffeted against the rocks, but somehow she managed, and then there was the welcome relief of Don's arms reaching her from behind. "I'll tow you in, OK?

Just lean back and relax."

She felt the powerful kick of his legs beneath her, and added her own paddle power, and within seconds they were safely on the beach, and Ellen was wringing the water from her hair. She was waiting for some sort of remark from Don, for surely this was too good a chance for him to miss of rubbing in the fact that she seemed to need a keeper. But instead he said, "Looks like you found the one weak spot in the beach. Must be a sort of whirlpool effect round the rocks."

"My own fault," Ellen admitted. "I let myself get out of condition — I thought I was a good swimmer. Lucky for me you came along."

Don smiled down at her. "Thank Selena for that. She saw you'd gone without putting sun cream on that fair skin of yours, so I brought it along to find you. Here, let me put some on."

Don's fingers massaged the cream into her bare shoulders, already stinging from their brief exposure to sun and salt. Ellen no longer felt self-conscious about her bikini; all her senses were focussed on the touch of his fingertips.

As they walked back to the others, Ellen was grateful that Don was not rubbing in, as well as the cream, the fact that for once she'd had to accept his help, had had no option to do otherwise. Instead he made light of her gratitude, and she knew he understood how shaken up she felt.

The morning drifted by in gentle conversation, dips in the sea, bottles of coke from the ice box. Gradually Ellen felt all the tension in her slowly uncoil and float away, and could see the same thing happening to Don. Lunch was leisurely, salad and cold meats in the cool of the house. Honor and Lee then declared that the fresh air had been too much for them, they were going to have a siesta. Sammy and Selena, on the other hand, decided to go into the nearest town.

When the others had gone, Don said,

"How do you feel now? Quite recovered?"

"Yes, thanks, though my arms still ache."

"Good. What do you want to do now? Fancy a drive? My car's in the garage."

Ellen hesitated. "I'd rather go for a walk," she said. "Unless you — ?"

"Me too," he said with enthusiasm. "We can follow the line of the dunes up to the point. They say there's a great view from there."

"This is idyllic," Ellen said as they set out. "I'm really glad Selena talked me into coming."

"She's a sweet kid," Don said. "I'm grateful Lee put me in touch with your uncle — he and Theresa have become my friends. Selena's like a second sister."

"I think she and Sammy are very much in love."

Don nodded. "Or so they think — I mean, Selena's not quite twenty, is she, and Sammy's just a bit older — so who knows what will happen next?"

"Not that young," Ellen disagreed. "I knew my mind when I was that age — and I'm sure you knew yours."

"Maybe about my career, but not about love and marriage. How could I? You don't have enough experience yet, and besides, people change."

"People can change whatever their age. There are no guarantees."

"Maybe not, but as you get more experience you can make a good guess, a better guess, about things like that."

"I don't think so — I think some people are better at that sort of thing than others. Some people can go through life making the same mistakes over and over."

"That's true — and I can promise you I'm not going to be one of them."

Ellen was taken aback by Don's fierce reply. "Why — did you think you were?"

But for answer Don stopped and looked out to sea; drew in a deep breath. "I don't know," he began, so unlike his usual decisive self and Ellen felt sure that he was about to tell her what was troubling him — but then, as before, he quickly hid his emotions and said, "I always feel that I'd like to stay on holiday for ever — until I've been away for a few days, then I begin to get restless again."

The smile had smoothed away the frown between his dark brows, the wind was ruffling his hair, curlier than usual after swimming, and in his old jeans and sweatshirt he seemed a long way from the sophisticated man about Wall Street with the razor sharp mind. Yet Ellen knew they were both the same man — the man she loved.

Then he put his arm casually across her shoulders, as if she was an old friend. "How come we always end up disagreeing with each other? Is it you or me who's so pig-headed?"

"Why you, of course, I'm entirely reasonable," Ellen said, eyes sparkling.

"Why no — if it's me you're talking about we'll call it strength of character — and just for that, I'll race you to that pine tree there!"

But although as usual he had evaded revealing any more of his inner thoughts,

Ellen felt closer to Don now than ever before.

That evening they prepared another barbecue. The smoke from the hickory chips scented the air, meat juices sizzled, their aroma mingling with the spices from a bowl of light fruit punch which Sammy and Selena had prepared.

Amid much hilarity they managed to carry out a large table from the kitchen on to the veranda and sat round it together to eat and talk, Sammy and Selena sitting close to each other and watching each other tenderly. Above, the stars gleamed in an immense black sky, and insects whined and buzzed in the cool night air, hurling themselves at the lights.

Ellen felt a great sense of peace. She wanted the day to go on for ever, and knew she would never forget it. The fresh air and all the day's activities combined to make her feel sleepy.

The next thing she knew she was being gently shaken awake. It was quiet, the others had all gone in, and the table was empty and wiped. Only Don was there, leaning over her, his hand on her shoulder.

"Wake up," he said. "I'd carry you up to your room but Honor and Lee forbade me to spoil you."

Just then someone inside the house switched off the garden lights and the stars seemed to sharpen their gleam, the wind to rustle more mysteriously in shadowy hollows. "I can't bear to think of going back to the city," Ellen whispered, almost to herself.

"Not go back?" Don held out his hand to help her to her feet and Ellen glimpsed again that expression she'd seen in his eyes when she'd woken. Was it tenderness? They were standing very close to each other in the darkness. "Do you mean that?"

Her answer died in her throat as, without conscious volition, their arms encircled one another and his lips were moving silkily across her forehead, her nose, her cheeks, and he pressed his hand against her hair. Ellen's skin felt on fire, and she held Don close, offering up her lips to his. Their mouths touched, gently, then again more urgently. The words 'I love you' were in her heart, in her mind, yet something held her back from speaking them.

When Don's face moved out of shadow into starlight, those translucent eyes of his could not lie to her. She could see the doubt in them, and knew she'd been right not to speak. Gently tracing a finger down her cheek, he said, "Ellen, you're so lovely, you'd tempt any man," but at the same time he was drawing away from her.

'I don't want any man,' she thought. 'I want you, only you.' But already he'd relinquished her and she shivered, suddenly cold outside the sheltering warmth of his arms.

"Forgive me, Ellen," he said.

Ellen didn't want to hear any more, but at least she'd salvage her pride.

"That's OK," she said lightly. "Put it down to a touch of the sun," and she went in, hoping he hadn't caught the slight tremble in her voice.

That was no exit line, she chided herself as she made her goodnights and went up to bed. If only she could have thought of something really snappy that would have put him in his place — twice now he'd kissed her, then backed off.

But as she tossed and turned the night away she knew why she'd done neither of those things. She'd escaped without having had to hear what she didn't want to hear, the reason for Don's behaviour, the truth she should have guessed at but hadn't wanted to, so deep were her feelings for him. Don must have made promises to another woman! He was clearly being sorely tempted by Ellen, but so far had managed to retain his control — just.

It was a conclusion, a truth, which plunged her in the deepest misery.

7

MONDAY morning. The long tedious drive back into New York City. In an unguarded moment Ellen had agreed to accept a lift from Don. Selena was staying on with Sammy and his parents for another few days, and Ellen envied her her freedom quite bitterly this morning, something she thought she'd never do. It was still early. Don had wanted to set off at half-past six to avoid the worst of the rush hour. He drove fast but safely, weaving in and out of the traffic in his low-slung Jaguar. Together they'd selected a light music channel on the car radio, and Ellen was glad for the melodies that filled the silence that now ached between them.

Even the sight of Manhattan's skyline in the distance, lurking under its layer of smog, didn't lift her spirits. She still had sand between her toes, both literally and figuratively. Her skin tingled from the light tan she'd acquired, her hair felt springy and wild from the salt water and wind, and her office clothes felt stiff and uncomfortable when she'd put them on this morning.

It wasn't just that she was leaving her holiday behind so soon, although that was part of it. Saturday had been idyllic, right up until the last moment when she'd read that mingled doubt and desire in Don's eyes. She'd dreaded the next day, arriving downstairs hollow-eyed and with a heavy heart. Fortunately, Lee and Honor had arranged a game of baseball in the scrubland behind the sand dunes, and she'd been able to immerse herself in that. Once or twice she'd caught Don's eyes on her, but determined not to show that her heart was breaking, she'd laughed even louder, flung herself after the ball more energetically, even walking out of a room to avoid him and noted, with what she knew was childish satisfaction, the way his face darkened.

Sunday night had been short, and she

saw that Don looked as if he had also lost some much needed sleep. Apart from brief remarks, they talked little during the journey. Don was, as usual, solicitous for her comfort, polite, but without his usual veneer of charm. Yet he was all the more attractive for his ragged exterior. She saw several women in other cars turn to look at him, and wondered yet again what the lucky woman who'd captured him was like.

It was her bad luck, she thought sourly but inconsistently, that she'd picked such an honourable man to fall in love with. He'd been tempted but he hadn't fallen. Nor had he encouraged Ellen to lose her heart to him. It must have been very difficult for him to resist someone who was so blatantly admiring him.

Suddenly he reached out and, with the closest she'd seen to a scowl on his face, said, "OK with you if I turn the radio off?"

"I don't mind — but that was the financial news just coming on. Don't you want to find out what's been going on?"

Frowning, concentrating on his driving, he said, "No thanks. If anything's happened worth talking about, we'll hear soon enough."

Obviously the break hadn't been long enough for him to get restless about work, Ellen thought. A short while later he parked his car in the car park beneath the Pepper Building.

"Well," he said, turning to look at her at last, "we're here."

"Right." Ellen was saddened by the fact that the easy closeness they'd shared had been shattered by that kiss. "So — thanks for the lift."

"I'll get your bag out of the boot." As he swung out their weekend bags and closed the boot, she could tell from the set of his shoulders that he had something to say to her. He took her hand. "Ellen, is everything all right?" His eyes searched her face. "Are you sure nothing's troubling you?"

Ellen stared at him in surprise. Could it possibly be that he didn't know, that he hadn't realised how she felt about him? And then she understood that he was asking her about Geiger Associates. Her heart thudded dismally, as she said, "Everything's fine," and then she made her escape.

She had been working for barely more than an hour before Maggie came across.

"So much news, I don't know where to start — and you spent the weekend with Don Redman after all, and you never breathed a word!"

"Wow, news travels fast around here. Who told you that? It's not really true, though."

"Barry was sorting out some papers in his briefcase, in the car park. Apparently he saw you holding hands with Redman, and you had suitcases. Barry told Yolande, the receptionist, and so it went on — everyone knows."

Ellen groaned. "It had to be Barry — and of course he misinterpreted what he saw." She explained what had happened, but not telling Maggie about the way Don had kissed her and the way he drew back.

"But Maggie, I'm sure he must have a girl friend, or somebody — it just didn't occur to me that we'd seen together like that, nor that everyone would gossip."

"No, you wouldn't think of that — but Don would. He didn't even try to be secretive," Maggie said thoughtfully. "Still, I guess he's got a lot on his mind at the moment."

"Why's that?"

"Didn't you hear? It hit the news-stands this morning — a massive fraud hundreds of thousands of clients' money misdirected. All small investors, and all put away in about six months, to buy shares in a company that doesn't exist! He made up a fictitious company, see, and he was about to get out — but he cut it too fine, and was discovered."

"That's incredible." Ellen shook her head. "But what's that got to do with Don?"

"Why, the guy worked here, at Geigers. There's going to be hell on today."

Ellen stiffened. She became aware now as she hadn't before, so wrapped up in her own thoughts had she been, that everyone was subdued, talking quietly or not at all. And then she remembered the paper Abrams had shown her had accused her of . . .

"Hy," she said, as Maggie nodded. "The man they got rid of so quickly just before I arrived — so Mr. Geiger must've known. But why keep it a secret for so long? And how did Mr. Geiger manage that?"

"I don't know — but Abrams was kept in the dark too. He was just told to fire Hy, and how to do it. He's been bellowing like an enraged bull all morning hadn't you noticed?"

Ellen gave a quick shake of her head. "No. And what you're saying is, that all this must be news to Don?"

"I don't know. Apparently Mr. Geiger managed to pull enough strings to keep it quiet because there's someone else involved — someone they haven't caught yet. Only a journalist managed to get hold of the story somehow, which is how it broke. And there's the money too — trying to get it back off Hy."

"I suppose Geigers are insured to cover the losses, to pay back the swindled people's money. But I wonder who the other person is? Any ideas?"

Maggie shook her head. "None — it could be anyone except for you and me and Mark of course. Hey, you're still looking distracted. How come you never noticed any of this?"

"Don turned off the car radio. He must've known the story was going to break today. As for distracted — Maggie, I'm afraid I've let my feelings for Don get the better of me. They're definitely not reciprocated. I know that for some strange reason he feels responsible for me, but as for anything else — forget it. And I'm sure there's someone else in his life."

"Oh Ellen, I'm sorry."

She forced a smile. "That's OK. I'll grow out of it, according to Don. But tell me about the party — how did it go? Did you see Ross?"

"The party — it was great. We had a

197

wonderful time, danced the night away."
As she spoke Maggie unconsciously turned
to look at Mark, and as if sensing her
eyes on him, Mark immediately looked
up and gave her a little wave. "As
for Ross — it was just like meeting
an old friend after a long time. No
problems at all."

"That's great. I'm really glad that my
letting you down like that over the
party — "

"You didn't let me down. In fact," and
she winked, "I think you may have done
me a good turn."

There was no further time to talk.
As the news began to spread about the
clever and massive fraud, people began to
ring up, asking for reassurance that their
money was safe, and some demanding
to change stockbrokers. Mr. Renkovic
and Mrs. Goldberg remained loyally
with Ellen, but several other people
requested to leave. Rumours abounded,
and one in particular revolved around
the speculation as to whether Mr. Geiger
had told CZR before they merged with

Geiger Associates. Supposing he'd kept it back, knowing that they would be able to cushion him from the severe after effects when the scandal was revealed? Or had he told all to Don Redman, who had still decided to go ahead with the merger even though Geiger Associates would be a liability rather than an asset?

Don had definitely known about it this morning when he'd deliberately avoided listening to the news. Had he also wanted to keep the facts from her? Clearly he had not relished the idea of discussing the fraud with her — or had it simply been a case of not wanting to get into the fray before it was absolutely necessary? She had no right to feel disappointed that he hadn't wanted to talk about it with her.

At home that evening she sat in front of the television eating omelette and chips, switching channels to catch the different newscasts. In one Ellen found what she wanted. Reporters were running after Don, having tracked him to the CZR building, as he made for a waiting limousine. Ellen felt a stab in her heart as she recalled his personal Jaguar sitting sleekly in the underground car park this morning. How much of his life he'd kept from her.

He was fending off reporters politely enough, but there was a cutting edge to his voice that showed he wasn't going to be pushed any further. At the door of the car he turned and said, as flash bulbs popped, "There will be a joint announcement shortly and until then I've nothing further to say." But Ellen was barely listening to his words. Her gaze was rivetted to the dark interior of the car, illuminated by those camera flashes, where a woman was sitting.

She was in her twenties, Ellen judged, with sleek black hair cut to curve into her jawline, and a short thick fringe. Her dark red lipstick outlined a full, generous mouth, and her large eyes glowed with life and amusement. As he got in she said something to Don and laughed, and just before the chauffeur closed the door on them Ellen saw her place a hand on Don's shoulder.

So that must be the woman Don really loved, to whom he was staying true! Ellen thought that actually seeing her, having her existence confirmed, would help her forget him, but the vision of her only etched itself deeper and deeper into her soul like burning acid.

She tried instead to concentrate on her speculation as to who Hy's accomplice might have been. Her first choice would be Abrams. Why else would he lash out at other people, if not to divert attention from his own shortcomings? Of course, he had singled Ellen out for his special attention, and not everyone saw him as she did, but she thought his accusation of her about those figures had surely been to use her as his scapegoat. Ellen was also aware that it was more a case of her wanting Abrams to be guilty.

Ellen slept badly that night, continually waking up with her mind revolving around Don, his girl friend, Abrams, the fraud. She was exhausted when she finally crawled into work the next day, and her weekend by the sea already seemed remote. The office buzzed with speculation, now the shock had worn off, and Ellen was pumped for information as to when an announcement was going to be made. She was glad she didn't know anything, because if she had she would have been tempted to tell all, just to get a breathing space. Fortunately, because this was not the first time her name had been linked with Don's, no one made any further specific remarks about her supposed weekend away with him.

It was Maggie who understood the significance to Ellen of the woman in Don's car.

"It could be another personal assistant," she suggested to cheer Ellen.

"No, it had to be his girl friend. I guessed all along that there had to be something, and after all, he only set out to protect me, he never hinted at anything else." She smiled bitterly. "Everyone here thinks that Don and I are having an affair, a relationship, when nothing could be further from the truth."

"But you know, I'm still puzzled about yesterday. Don knows the score, so why has he allowed these rumours to circulate — they might get back to his girl friend, for one thing."

"I guess it wasn't a priority to him at the time — and we were both foolish not to remember how gossip spreads."

It was Ellen's turn now to receive one of those head-hunting telephone calls from a rival firm. Rosaleen worked for a financial company that equalled CZR in size, and Ellen was very flattered that it wasn't just an agency that had called her. She'd met Rosaleen at a financial conference.

"Apart from being impressed when we met," she said, "I've heard that you're able to handle difficult clients, and we're on the look — out for exactly that kind of person. The fact that a client may be small, and perhaps not easy to get along with, doesn't mean we should lose them. We want to cater for everybody."

"Well, I don't know where you found all this out about me," Ellen said, amazed at Rosaleen's information — gathering skills, and wondering whether it stretched to her supposed relationship with Don too. "But I'm not sure that I really want to specialise along the lines you're suggesting."

"Of course not. You'd be able to take on whoever you wanted, but you must see that it's a big plus on your side. So the very minute you, feel you'd like a change of routine, call me. I'll be waiting to hear from you."

Although she didn't tell Rosaleen, Ellen found herself tempted to leave for the first time. Geigers was no longer the place she'd started working for. Everything had changed and was upside-down. Many of the familiar faces were disappearing, to be replaced by strangers, and more were thinking of it. And then she had Abrams breathing down her neck at every opportunity, with no sign that war was to cease. Added to that she was in love with Don Redman. Moving to another company would solve all her problems at once. The more she thought about it, the more attractive the idea seemed.

Her feelings of loyalty were at war with her desire to escape, to start afresh, anything to break her out of this emotional whirlpool. She would have liked to talk it over with someone, but everyone had their own problems. In fact, the person she'd most like to discuss it with was Don. But for once he was the last person she could approach, would ever approach.

Later that afternoon, during a quiet period, Mark came over to her, a serious look on his face, and pulled a chair close to her desk.

"Ellen, I'd like to have a talk. Can you spare a moment?"

Alarmed, Ellen said, "Sure, any time. What's it all about?"

Mark hesitated. "It's about Don Redman. I know you've denied that you're having a — a relationship, but you can't deny that — well — if you wanted to, you could approach him. Is that right?"

Ellen conceded the point. "But then, so could anyone here. He's not a machine, you know. Your gossip was quite wrong, he doesn't have a dollar sign on his heart," and she surprised herself by her vehemence.

Mark leaned closer and said quietly, "In that case, I've got a chance. Can you speak to him about me? I'm feeling so kinda held back. I mean, I don't want to move on, but I really feel it's time I moved up. Know what I mean?"

Ellen spread her hands helplessly. "I don't know what you want me to do."

"Look, I intend to make it to the top, and I mean the very top, just like Redman has. But you know what Abrams is like. No one can get past him. He's got us bottle-necked here. I like Geigers, I'm willing to stay, though everyone else is leaving — and that'll be better for me, because I'll know the ropes. But I've got to have prospects, see?"

"You want me to deliver a kind of ultimatum, then, is that it? Either you get promoted or you join the mass exodus?" Ellen said slowly. "But why don't you tackle Don yourself? Anyway, this isn't the best time to add fresh problems to those he already has."

Mark moved uneasily in his seat. "I wouldn't put it quite like that, but it's been preying on my mind recently. I want to know which way to jump next, and who knows better than Redman? What's more, I want it to happen soon. He's got a couple of years on me, but I've got a lot of catching up to do. And don't you see, the fact that this is a difficult time is exactly why I've come to you."

"You're very impatient, Mark."

"Sure I am. You can't hang around in this game, or people trample on you." He laid his hand over Ellen's and smiled his boyish smile. "So can you do that for me, huh? It'd mean a lot to me — and to Maggie too, I guess."

"I'll think about it, Mark." He had to add that mention of Maggie, she

207

thought, to soften her up. His smile had looked so false to her, and she felt a great sadness. Had this been what his friendship was all about all along? She remembered that his first interest in her had coincided with the exact moment he'd overheard her talking about Don. Such naked ambition! Don had been right, he'd warned her about it right at the start. Not that Mark had cheated, exactly. Most people would think he was doing the right thing, pulling a string. Only she hated the idea that Don was considered vulnerable through someone like her. Her instinct was to defend him at any cost.

She looked across at Maggie's dark, sleek head, and her heart twisted. Would Maggie think it right that she should speak to Don on Mark's behalf? Or would she think it sneaky? Mark's feelings for Maggie had to be genuine. Maggie wasn't someone he could use. But perhaps she should warn her anyway. A gentle hint, to make sure that her friend wasn't let down badly if it should happen.

But she shouldn't interfere. It was up to Maggie to make up her own mind about Mark. Ellen had spent a lot of time explaining that very point to Don, and it was unlikely that Maggie would want to hear negative things about Mark. She would probably defend him, just as Ellen had defended Don.

It was agonising trying to work out what course of action she should take. Her friend might be in danger of another heartache, and Ellen didn't know whether to warn her or leave it all to Fate.

She grimaced wryly. This must have been how Don felt when he first met her, fresh from England's shores, and looking so bewildered and unsure of herself. It had been his decision to try to talk to her, and she had been completely ungrateful.

Perhaps Mark's request wasn't so bad after all. She only had to pass on the fact that he was feeling restless. But no, he'd definitely hoped she might soften Don up on his behalf. She frowned. If only he'd kept quiet, she might well have told Don, quite spontaneously, about him and how good he was at his job — but then, wasn't her argument with herself quite redundant? She wasn't going to be having any more cosy chats with Don Redman, least of all the sort where he would immediately demand to know why Mark had come to her in the first place.

It wouldn't take Don long to find out how much gossip there'd been about the two of them, and then he'd want to know why she hadn't shared that problem with him. Ellen sighed and tapped away at her computer. This was no good. She was caught in the coils of a maze, and had no idea which was the right way out.

She did try to broach the subject of Mark to Maggie. They were in the Dice Bar together, drinking cool fruit juice, filling in time while Maggie was waiting for Mark to join her before they went out to dinner. Outside the sky was cloudy and droplets of rain filled the sultry air, while in the distance thunder growled softly.

"I can still hardly believe what's happening between us," Maggie was saying, almost shyly. "Looking back I realise I was dreading seeing Ross again, but now I can't think why. I think I'd got used to feeling sorry for myself which is fatal. Being with Mark seemed so natural, and we have our work in common too."

"Mark's very ambitious, I think," Ellen said carefully. "I expect he talks to you about his plans for the future."

"He wants the best things in life, and you can't blame him for that, can you?"

Ellen shook her head. "But he seems so carefree on the surface. I wonder if he's really ruthless enough — or perhaps he's hiding all that underneath!" Ellen added jokingly, to see what Maggie's reaction would be.

"Oh no, not Mark," she said firmly. "He's not cold and calculating — though he does take risks."

"I'm sorry, I can see you're jumping

to his defence. It's just that — perhaps this has all happened very suddenly. I'm only worried in case you get hurt again, that's all."

"Thanks, Ellen. But really, Mark isn't a case of the rebounds. It's been a long time since Ross — but I know now that was only because nobody else had come along. And now they have."

The insistent shrilling of the telephone dragged Ellen from sleep. She'd dozed off after eating her supper, and the record on the stereo had long since finished playing, the soothing music having lulled her into much-needed sleep after her recent broken nights. It was Aunt Theresa, her rich voice expressing amusement at Ellen's sleepy tones.

"It's not you young one's who're supposed to nod off in front of the TV. Have you been burning the candle at both ends or shouldn't I ask?"

"It's mainly work. So much has been happening here." She explained about the fraud. "And with all the publicity, instead of getting on with the job, we're having to answer people's questions and so on," she concluded.

"Poor Don. It sounds like he's taken on more than he bargained for. What does he say about all this?"

"I don't know, Aunt Theresa, I haven't spoken to him since the weekend — did you know he was coming to Sammy's parents too?" Ellen asked, a faint suspicion forming at the back of her mind, but her Aunt's voice was innocent enough.

"No, honey, but that must've been a fun time — and that's one of the reasons I'm calling you. I haven't been able to raise Selena since you came back."

"No, she stayed on with Sammy — I think she said she was sending you a postcard. It was beautiful up there, and of course with Sammy there too — I wish I could've stayed on. She's lucky."

Her aunt caught something in her voice she hadn't realised was there.

"You sound down, honey. Not letting the job get to you, I hope?"

Ellen knew she could pour her heart

out to her aunt in a way she couldn't with her mother, who would only worry. But Don was Aunt Theresa's stockbroker as well as friend, and it wouldn't be right to discuss him with her. Instead she said, "No, only I'm thinking of changing jobs. It's not the fraud so much as — well, someone who goes out of his way to make life difficult for me."

"But you shouldn't have to leave because of that. It sounds unfair to me. What exactly has he done? Shouldn't you talk it over with someone?"

Ellen recognised this as sound advice. However, only she knew that Abrams wasn't her real reason for leaving. "I don't know. It's more complicated than that — so many changes . . . "

"I think you ought to discuss it with Don — you mustn't be too proud to ask for help. Or would you like me to call him?"

"No! No, thanks, Aunt Theresa. I'll find out more about the job I've been offered, I promise, first."

"That's a start. But remember what

I said. You don't have to shoulder whatever it is that's troubling you alone. But the best of luck in whatever you decide to do."

Ellen replaced the receiver thoughtfully. Not to have to shoulder anything alone, to have someone to share her troubles, someone she could trust — no, that way temptation lay. She had to make up her own mind about whether to leave or not, whether it was better to stand and fight, or cut her losses.

Then the phone rang again and she lifted the receiver automatically, so immersed was she in her thoughts. It was Don, and he was using a pay phone. She could hear cheerful clatter and music in the background.

"Ellen, there's something I must discuss with you — I'm down here in Arnaldi's Deli. Can you come and meet me now?"

Ellen quickly combed her hair, then made her way nervously downstairs, calling out as she crossed the lobby, "Evening Joe. How are you?"

"Just fine, Miss Huntsworth. But where

you off to at this time of night?"

"Arnaldi's," she informed him with a smile.

"The place to be. I just saw Mr. Redman going in there — aha!" he grinned and winked. "Don't worry, your secret's safe with me."

There was an empty coffee cup in front of Don, and he'd taken off his jacket and draped it on the back of the chair, leaving him in his white shirt, open at the neck. Ellen was shocked to see how different he looked from when she'd last seen him. Then he'd been tanned, relaxed, but now his features were tense and drawn, accentuating the lines on either side of his mouth, making his nose more prominent. But he managed a warm smile when he saw her, relieving the worst of his drawn expression. "How are you, Ellen? Let me get you some coffee — would you prefer tea?"

"Well — I'd love some ice-cream."

"You know all Arnaldi's specialities! Italian ice-cream." He spoke to the waitress, then looked back at Ellen, his eyes searching her face. "You don't look too mad at me," he said at last.

"Mad at you? Why, what have you done?"

"Maybe the rumours haven't reached you yet, but they have me. You're still looking blank — haven't you heard?"

"What rumours?" Ellen asked, her heart beating fast in alarm.

"We were seen arriving together the other morning, and two and two were made to add up to eleven — how come you haven't heard?"

"Oh, that. Yes, the gossip spread very fast, and I've denied it. It isn't the first time our names have been connected."

"I'm sorry, Ellen, that you're being put through all this." He ran a hand through his hair. "The only thing I can do is say nothing. Denial, comment, will only inflame the gossip — believe me, I know. It should turn out to be a two day wonder. If you get any problems, refer them to me." He paused. "I was too careless — it was my fault."

Ellen shrugged. "It was no one's fault, and it isn't causing me — well, anyway, you must've been preoccupied, and I was just — OK, I admit it, naïve. Anyway, we know the truth, so who cares?"

"That's fighting talk, and I wouldn't expect anything less from you. But I've let you down — I promised to take care of you when I could."

"I promise you, I can take it — but isn't it far more dangerous for you?"

Don shrugged. "My back's broad. I can take it, too."

"Yes, but you don't have only yourself to consider, not like me."

His glance was sharp. "You may be right. I hadn't thought of that before. But there'll be consequences for you too, and I'm glad they haven't reached you yet."

Ellen ate some of the ice-cream from the end of the long spoon before replying. "I don't really — I mean it won't — " and Don swooped on her hesitation.

"Something has happened, I can tell. Out with it, Ellen."

"Um, not exactly. Only some people

think — have hinted — that perhaps I can use my influence with you. On their behalf. Only I haven't."

"Darn it, that's the last thing I wanted to happen." He ran a hand through his hair again, wearily. "What did they want you to do?"

"Recommend them, praise them, that sort of thing." She paused. "It's so difficult to tell whether you can really trust someone, or whether they — well, they want to use you."

"You've been hurt. I can tell that too. Ellen, I would've done anything to save you from this." He reached out a hand and touched hers.

"You tried, but I'm certainly learning fast from the experience." She smiled, enjoying the weight of his hand on hers.

"There must be a solution to all this — I'm glad you told me. Now I'll be able to work something out."

Ellen swallowed. "There is one answer. I can leave Geiger Associates." She stopped, halted by the flash in Don's eyes, but he didn't say anything. "I've been offered another job — who hasn't? And I'm trying to decide what to do."

Don withdrew his hand and frowned down at his coffee cup. "You're obviously attracted to the idea, and I guess you'll have investigated it thoroughly. You've got quite a decision to make there."

"I know," Ellen said quietly. "I should be sorry to leave Geiger Associates, but so much has happened, it's beginning to feel uncomfortable."

"Ellen, you have to make up your own mind on this, you know that, and I won't try to influence you one way or another. Apart from this — you must not leave if it's simply the gossip that's upsetting you, because I shall put a stop to that. You've told me it isn't bothering you too much, but perhaps you're trying to spare my feelings?"

"No, I've told you the truth. It's a complicated set of reasons."

"Well then, I should be sorry to see you go, but I know you'll choose what's best for you."

"Thanks." Ellen pushed her ice-cream to one side sadly. She wasn't talking to Don, her friend, but Mr. Redman, her boss. The gap between them seemed to have widened, and there didn't seem to be anything else for her to say.

8

ELLEN slept surprisingly well that night, but woke early. She knew the instant she opened her eyes that she'd made her decision. Somewhere, perhaps in a dream, it had come to her in her sleep. She had to cut her losses and leave Geiger Associates. Her love for Don had to be overcome, because in her case familiarity was breeding the opposite of contempt. She had to remove herself from his orbit.

She had not expected him to make some wild demonstration of his feelings for her and persuade her to stay. That hadn't been the reason she'd discussed it with him. On the other hand she'd been very surprised that, when for the first time she'd actively asked for his advice, he had not leapt at the opportunity of giving it to her. Instead he'd gone out of his way not to influence her. It was a completely different Don from the one she'd first met. She refused to contemplate the idea that he simply didn't care enough. It hurt too much.

Ellen phoned Rosaleen first to confirm that the job was still there, then to accept it. Rosaleen was delighted. "This is fantastic news," she said. "I hope you can soon start."

"I hope so too — no one likes prolonged changeovers here, there's too much at stake. I'll try to be with you in a couple of weeks."

"Good. Let me know, and everything'll be ready. I promise you, you won't regret your decision."

Ellen stared at the phone once she'd rung off. It was as easy as that. The route she was taking now would be as important as the one that had led her across the Atlantic in the first place, most probably, but she felt none of the excitement and anticipation of that first move, only a dull ache where her heart should be. Ellen handed in her written resignation to Karen, Abrams' secretary, next, simply stating that she'd accepted another job, and wanted to leave in a fortnight. To her dismay Abrams asked her to come and see him almost immediately. Did he intend to gloat, she wondered? She looked at Karen enquiringly, but she just shook her head. "So, what's all this about?" he asked, tapping her letter. "The pace at Geigers too much for you? Got problems?" As usual, he sounded impatient, but his tone wasn't his customary belligerant one. She fixed her gaze just to one side of his eyes and said, "I was made a good offer, and decided to accept it."

"More money, huh? Is that it? Did nobody tell you we have an annual salary review at Christmas — probationary salary. There's usually a year's end bonus, too. Don't say you think Geigers is not generous."

"No, it's not that. The money here's fine. Only I just — wanted a change."

Ellen was taken aback by what Abrams was saying. It was hard to tell with him, but it almost sounded as if he was trying to tempt her to stay.

"A change. You girls are all the same — new wardrobe, new hairstyle, new job — no, I'm only kidding." He raised his hand as she opened her mouth to protest. "No, I can understand itchy feet, happens to all of us. Only you've got to learn to tell when it's a passing phase and when it's the genuine thing, know what I mean?"

Ellen nodded. She realised that he was genuinely puzzled. He had no idea why she was leaving. "It's definitely the genuine thing. So can I take it you've accepted? And can I go in two weeks?"

"Take it, take it — no, you may not take it." He was becoming agitated. "I want you to have a cooling off period — come see me in a week's time, OK?" He paused. "I mean, what did Mr. Redman say about this sudden change of heart?"

Now Ellen understood it all. He was anxious in case she'd talked about his unfair treatment of her with either Don or Mr. Geiger. "I won't be changing my mind," she said, "and I'll go ahead and make my plans accordingly."

"OK, OK," he said, almost reasonably. "But keep an open mind. Your job's here until you actually go — remember that."

"Thanks — I will."

Ellen walked thoughtfully back to her desk. She'd seen Abrams in a new light. He'd been afraid, and although he hadn't said as much, she'd just received the nearest thing to an apology from him she was likely to get.

"Ellen, what's up with you today? You look so preoccupied, and now you're with Abrams. What gives?"

"Oh Maggie, I'm sorry — I've just been arranging that new job. I've decided to take it — only I will miss you."

"And I'll miss you — but I'm so happy for you. I'm sure you're making the right decision — but you don't look very pleased about it. What is it, Abrams again? Aren't you glad you'll be seeing the last of him?"

"Abrams didn't react at all like I expected," Ellen replied glumly. "In fact, I think he felt he'd gone too far in the past. No, it isn't him. It's Don. I've got to get out, start afresh."

"Oh Ellen — I'm sorry. You need cheering up, and I wish I could take you to lunch, only I'm already booked up."

"Lunch, lunch? Who's hungry already? It's not ten o'clock," Mark said, joining them. Maggie explained what had happened, while Ellen struggled with her mixed feelings towards Mark.

"You've got to celebrate," Mark said. "I'll take you out — I'm free."

"That's a good idea," Maggie agreed. "Mark'll make sure you shake this mood."

Ellen's unusually lack-lustre acceptance of Mark's offer was clearly put down by Maggie to Ellen's general mood of despondency. Because Maggie had been so keen for her to go, she hadn't wanted to refuse — it would have been too obvious she wanted to avoid Mark.

They went to the Dice Bar, which offered light lunches, and he insisted on treating her to a King Prawn salad and, despite her protests, ordered a bottle of champagne.

"Hey, Ellen, don't take it so hard," he said. "You really look down — but we'll still be seeing as much of you as ever. And this will be a great opportunity for you. It's a good place you've chosen to go to."

"I know. You're right." Dutifully she drank some of her champagne and arranged her features in an unconvincing smile.

"In fact, Ellen, I'm glad Maggie can't be with us right now — you remember yesterday I asked you to do me a favour?"

Ellen nodded. So this was why he'd been keen to take her out — he wanted to pump her for information, find out if she'd talked to Don yet. But his next words restored her faith in him immediately.

"I hope you haven't done anything about it — I know you said you were going to think about it; only now," he fiddled awkwardly with his cutlery, "now I wish I'd never said anything in the first place. I shouldn't've asked it of you. I guess I was starting to live in the future, and wanted to make things happen quickly." He shot her a glance from his light blue eyes. "I'm really serious about Maggie. I guess you know that, and I — well, I want to go places, do well for the both of us, only I overshot myself."

"It's a real relief to hear you say that — and I'm so pleased for you and Maggie."

"Thanks — one thing though. Promise you won't tell Maggie? She'd think me a real heel, and I already think that myself."

Ellen felt her spirits lifting. "I promise — and why don't you pour me another glass of that lovely champagne. It's not every day I'm given such a treat."

The next day everyone who worked at Geiger Associates was summoned to a meeting, to be held at six in the evening to avoid too much disruption. Geiger and Redman signed a joint memo saying that they wanted to read out their prepared announcement. As everyone poured into the small conference chamber it soon became crowded, and people had to sit on the floor and line the walls. Harold Geiger entered first, waving in his usual relaxed manner, but Ellen was sure he must be aware of the hostile feelings towards him in the room. People wanted to be reassured, and they wanted their questions answered — especially why he'd chosen to cover up the fraud, so that the first they'd heard had been from a newspaper.

Then Don came in. Tall and tanned, his suit as usual fitting like a second skin. Ellen studied him, for once, from far away, as if he was someone she hadn't met before, but found that those strong features, the piercing eyes, the grey flecked hair, with its unruly tendency to curl, held her as much in thrall as ever. She couldn't help but feel anxious for him. This was bound to be a difficult meeting. But when Mr. Geiger had introduced him, and Don had stood up to read out the announcement, and then had pushed aside his papers, leaned one hand on the wooden lectern, and begun to speak conversationally to his audience, Ellen realised that she didn't have to worry. Don soon had them all well on his side.

"You'll all hear the official line shortly, so I want to give you the background to all this. I've admired Geiger Associates for a long time for its independence and honesty. When Harold came to me and told me that through his own vigilance he'd uncovered a massive fraud, we talked, and decided that a merger was the answer to the problems that would follow. CZR was big enough to absorb the punches, while in the long term, far from it being an act of charity, CZR would benefit from being associated with such a prestigious company. So, now you know the background, I'll read the statement. Any questions so far?"

"Just one," a voice called out, amid murmurs of agreement. "Why wait so long before telling us?"

"We had to complete our investigation — and as it was, the news leaked out early. But it's completed now."

There was an instant stir. Heads turned, eyes searched. The co-conspirator had been discovered, but who was it?

"Clyde," she heard Maggie whisper. "Where's Clyde? Remember he wasn't around at all yesterday either?"

Ellen nodded. Clyde. That made sense. He'd been Hy's close friend — and now she thought about it, her theory that Abrams had picked on her to deflect interest in himself, applied even more so to Clyde. It was mainly due to him that she'd had such a cold reception from her colleagues.

Other questions followed. What was going to be the future of Geiger Associates? Could Don guarantee that it would stay the same size, or would some people lose their jobs? Sometimes Don answered, sometimes Harold Geiger, and Ellen could almost feel sorry that she was leaving, now that the new shape of Geiger Associates was emerging. But if she had any doubts, all she had to do was look at Don and know that, as long as he made her feel the way she did about him, the further she removed herself from him the better.

Ellen's remaining days at Geiger Associates passed slowly, and continued to be full of heart-searching and misgivings. Gradually she put everything in order, informed her clients — and was moved when people like Mr. Renkovic and Mrs. Goldberg were very upset to hear the news — and prepared herself for the change. It made her realise just how deeply she had entrenched herself in her job in such a short space of time, especially when the other stockbrokers, in complete contrast to when she'd arrived, actually seemed sorry that she was leaving.

But although she was surrounded by good will, and was looking forward to the challenge of her new job, she still wondered if she'd made her decision too hastily. She ought to be planning whether it was a good career move, and instead she was allowing her emotions to rule her head. And just as often she told herself that any reluctance to go on her part was only because she still clung to some faint hope that one day Don could reciprocate her feelings. She knew that to be absolutely sure of herself she needed to find a new apartment too, but was putting that off for now.

On Friday evening she arrived home late, having been shopping, which included a last stop at the supermarket which was situated half a block away. She carried two large brown paper bags in her arms, full of household goods and an odd selection of food for the weekend. She was so preoccupied these days that she couldn't even plan a straightforward menu. It had been a long and tedious day; a thundery August downpour had started as soon as she'd left the supermarket and it had been impossible to find a taxi for such a short distance, so she was uncomfortably wet.

She entered the lobby ready to unload her woes on sympathetic Joe, as usual on his evening duty this week, but stifled her voice immediately, and turned to one side, pretending to rearrange her shopping. Talking to Joe was Don's girl friend. Her black hair shone glossily, and her smart safari-style summer clothes showed off her neat figure. Ellen heard her say goodbye and, head down and eyes averted, she prepared to pass her — when the bottoms of both bags burst, having been soaked by the rain, cascading tins and packages on to the floor.

"Oh, what bad luck," Don's girl friend said sympathetically and bent to help her pick them up, while Joe went to find her another bag. "Look, here're your eggs. I don't think they're broken."

"No — and thanks, that was — very kind," Ellen muttered, annoyed to find that Don's girl friend appeared to be so nice.

"You're welcome," she said, and was gone, leaving a faint, lingering scent in the air, musky but not cloying.

"Here you are, Miss Huntsworth. This'll hold 'em."

"That's great, Joe." Together they began to pile all her goods into the bag, then Ellen asked, "Joe — who was that?"

He looked at her in surprise. "Why, that's Annabel. But I thought you of all people would know that." And he winked again. Ellen wished he wouldn't. There wasn't much you could say to a wink.

"Well, thanks. Good night, Joe."

So her name was Annabel. Numbly Ellen put her from her mind and concentrated on getting her key out to open her front door. She was relieved to be home at last, looking forward to kicking off her shoes, putting all her shopping away, and shutting her door on the world for the evening. She intended to have a long bath, relax with a book and have an early night.

She stood transfixed in her doorway by the sight that awaited her. The room seemed to be filled with bouquets of

236

flowers — yet she couldn't have opened the wrong door. Exclaiming with delight Ellen turned from roses to freesias, to carnations, their delightful scent filling the air. Unexpectedly, tears pricked her eyes. What a lovely surprise — but who? Why?

She caught sight of a card on the table — it was a birthday card. Birthday! How could she have forgotten her own birthday? Tomorrow she would be twenty-four, and she'd simply erased that fact from her mind. But her parents had remembered and organised this. She hurried to put down her bags, then went to pick up the card, trying to blot out memories of family gatherings for birthdays, candles on a cake made by her mother, the family jokes ... she blinked the tears away.

Quickly she flicked open the card — and then her heart almost stopped for a second. It said, simply, *"Don"*. She looked around again in wonderment. Had he arranged this? Surely not — the idea was quite crazy — then she understood.

It surely must be on behalf of her aunt and uncle. She hadn't mentioned her birthday, had forgotten it, but her parents must have spoken to them, and they'd asked him to organise it.

The doorbell sounded. She wasn't expecting anyone, so she stood by the door and called out, "Who is it?" while peering through the fish-eye lens. All she saw was a dark shoulder. "It's Don. Can I come in?"

"Oh — Don — I — " Ellen looked down at herself. Stockings splashed by traffic, hair limp — she was a mess, especially when compared with the beautiful Annabel. "I'm in the middle of a shower right now — but thank you Don. The flowers are beautiful," she called through the door. "I'll phone Aunt Theresa and thank her."

"What was that you said? Theresa?"

"That's right. I said I'd — "

"Look, this is ridiculous. We can't spend all night talking through a door. I want to invite you to dinner. When are you free — tonight?"

"Tonight! Yes, I'm free." And for the rest of my life, she added silently.

The restaurant was everything the cheerful Italian one he'd taken her to had not been. In the background was the faint, almost discordant twang of the Japanese *samisen*. Paper screens delicately painted with brightly coloured birds and large chrysanthemums separated the tables from each other. Set in the ceramic tiles of the floor were small pools containing goldfish, with one perfect water lily in each. It was utterly tranquil.

The overhead lighting was subdued, and on their low table burned a small night-light. Their waitress brought their food on silent feet, her appearances as unobtrusive as possible. The food itself, in tiny portions, was neatly arranged on the plate with an eye for colour as well as pattern. Don and Ellen sat cross-legged on cushions on the floor, having discarded their shoes at the door.

"You must try the raw fish," Don was

urging her. "It's delicious when you dip it into this sauce here."

Carefully Ellen manoeuvred her chopsticks and captured a small piece of fish, dipped it, then put it into her mouth. To her surprise, he was right.

"Now for the *sake.*" His long tapering fingers dwarfed the tiny porcelain cups as he poured out the warmed rice wine. "Ellen — to your health and happiness!"

Ellen sipped the powerful drink, then put her cup down. It was now or never. So far Don had been infuriatingly non-committal. He'd admitted only that the flowers were his own idea. He knew it was her birthday some time this weekend, and determined to help her celebrate it. He had been courteous and charming, and was breaking her heart. She knew she'd been weak to come, weak to agree to share her birthday with him. He only had to snap his fingers and she came running. But there had to be more to it. Why had Don dismissed Annabel on a Friday evening, and then casually invited out his neighbour?

"Don — you must tell me. Why all this? And when's the rest of the party going to arrive?"

"Party? There's no one else, just the two of us."

"Don, you're avoiding my eyes — look at me straight and tell me this isn't part of a surprise, and any minute my aunt and uncle and Selena will be coming in."

He looked up then, and Ellen felt her insides turning molten as his grey eyes seemed to penetrate to her innermost being. He gently shook his head.

Ellen was bewildered. "But — why? The flowers, and this, it's lovely but — why are you doing it?"

He leaned forward and gently curled a tendril of her hair around his finger. "I'm doing it because it's what I want — at last. And because for once I listened to Annabel."

"Annabel? But — but I saw her today, this evening, and she looked very happy."

"So she is. She doesn't have any reason not to be, not now." He paused in his examination of her hair. "And Abrams helped make up my mind for me, too. Ellen, I haven't told you how beautiful you are. There are golden lights in your eyes, and the way your mouth curves is just perfect."

Ellen was dumbfounded. Don was saying all the things she'd longed to hear — and it was because of Annabel? And Abrams?

"Don't you care how Annabel feels?" she demanded.

"Now those golden lights are glinting, just as they always do when you're mad," he was smiling infuriatingly calmly. "I seem to have seen them like that an awful lot of the time. I can't think why. As for Annabel, of course I care, and I love my sister just as much as ever."

"Your — *sister* — but I thought — " Ellen's eyes glinted even more, even though Don's fingers were now lightly resting on her cheek. "But when you kissed me you said — and I believed — "

Don sat up in surprise. "But I thought you knew. I'm sure I told you I had a sister. I never intended you to think otherwise." His gaze softened. "I can understand now why you abandoned me on the veranda that night. I wanted to explain, but you stormed off and refused to be alone with me. By Monday morning I was angry enough myself, and decided that if that was the way you wanted to play it, so be it. That was a nightmare, that journey. You were sitting so close to me, yet there didn't seem to be any way to bridge the gap between us."

"And all the time I thought you were thinking about your work — specially afterwards, when the fraud story broke that day." She paused. "Well, I'm not storming off anywhere now." She smiled. "I guess we were both being pig-headed."

His eyes searching her face as she spoke, Don said, "Annabel's two years older than you. She wanted to follow me into the financial world, and that was fine by me. I encouraged and helped her, coached her. I guess I was acting like a father as well as brother, since our parents died. Does that make sense?"

Ellen nodded. "Of course."

"I felt responsible for her because I'd actively encouraged her. What I didn't take into account was, as I was already involved in big deals and considered a primary target, one way to get to me was through Annabel."

"You mean — the sharks got her?" Ellen asked, dismayed.

"That's right. One shark in particular. He was an expert conman, pretended he was rich and powerful and wasn't interested in me. He dazzled her, asked her to marry him — then at the last moment he beat me on a particularly important deal, scooped a lot of money, ditched her, and there was nothing we could do. She'd passed on information voluntarily, not realising the consequences, and she didn't want to sue him for the broken engagement. Annabel was shattered, went wild for a while. The newspapers got hold of some stories and blew them up out of all proportion, gave her a notoriety she didn't deserve."

"And you felt responsible for that?"

"I tried to warn her. He was attractive

enough, but instinct told me not to trust him. The more I opposed her relationship with him, the more it drove her into his arms. It was frustrating to know I was right, but I couldn't do anything about it." He looked away for a moment, then flicked his gaze back to her face. "I didn't tell you the full story for that reason — you were already fiercely independent, and I felt the more I pressed you, the more you'd do the opposite — just like she did."

"What's changed you now? You said Annabel — and Abrams? But what's he got to do with us?"

Don poured them some more *sake.* "Abrams came to see me, stricken with guilt — as far as you can tell with him. He's like a rock outside, and all putty inside. He told me he'd been too hard on you, and that I should persuade you not to leave."

"He was against me before I even arrived; I don't know why."

"He explained to me — he wouldn't to you, a woman. He hoped that Mr. Geiger would give his son a start, but instead he took you on, and asked Abrams to be especially helpful to you, which made him react badly."

"I could almost feel sorry for him now," Ellen said. "What will happen to him?"

"A severe reprimand, and I'm fitting his son into CZR." Don fixed her with a stern eye. "You didn't tell me any of this, but I realised that you'd coped with Abrams; swung him round in your favour. And you coped with the gossip about the two of us — and I understood then that being protective towards you was more or less unnecessary. You proved you could look after yourself, and I had to re-examine my feelings towards you. When you asked me about your new job I'd had the sense not to try to influence you, and after my interview with Abrams, it became imperative not to say anything — but I hated the idea of losing even that contact with you." He captured her hands in his. "I'm trying to tell you how I feel about you. I've become too obsessively secretive about my private life, and you can see why, but perhaps I can show you . . . "

He stroked her fingers tenderly, then took each one and kissed it in turn, till Ellen wanted to cry out with happiness. Then the waitress interrupted them, bringing them a light, savoury stew in small, cast-iron pots, from which the steam curled lazily up. Ellen rescued her fingers, tried to hide her blushes and asked, "How is Annabel now?"

"Great. She runs her own small business, and those two years of hell are fading fast — that was just before I met your aunt and uncle, so they know nothing about any of this."

"I understand," Ellen said thoughtfully. "When you saw me, naïve and dewy-eyed, you thought I might be another Annabel."

Don grimaced and put down his spoon. "I think I wanted to save you from me. I was wildly attracted to you — but you were in the same business as me, and all I could see were problems because of that. Sure, when I first saw you I thought you needed protection, but I think I was kidding myself even then." He smiled tenderly. "It was hard at your aunt and uncle's party though. You looked so delectable that evening."

"I remember you warning me about danger — after we had dinner together. And you said you wouldn't make the same mistakes again." Ellen looked down. "I knew how I felt about you, but I was so determined to prove I could make it on my own, I would have walked away from you into another job, another apartment." She shuddered. "And I was warned — by Maggie and Selena."

"Well, let's drink to Annabel and Abrams and all our friends who've finally made us see some sense — but you're not eating with your usual healthy appetite. Perhaps a Japanese restaurant was the wrong idea."

"No, no, it's beautiful; it's only that this feels like a dream. I'm not sure I didn't faint on my doorstep, and I'm imagining all this."

"Here, take my hand does that feel real enough?"

Ellen clung to it, pressed it against her cheek. It was good to know he was there, someone to support her, someone she could love without reserve.

"You know, I already knew that you could take care of yourself before. That day you showed me round — even though I was your new boss, and I'd made a special request for you to help me, you had no reservations in telling me exactly what you thought." He grinned. "I began to think my case was hopeless, but I couldn't keep away from you, had to ask you out to. dinner."

"You asked! But Abrams didn't tell me. I thought it was another trick of his to belittle me. If I'd known I'd never have said — "

"My little wildcat," Don said affectionately, refusing to let go of her hand. "I'm sure you'd have given your honest opinion just the same. But you see, I not only wanted to be with you — I knew

I could trust only you, when there was someone there at Geigers who couldn't be trusted."

"I wanted you to tell me what was going on, but you didn't discuss any of it with me," Ellen told him, "so I felt you were saying — I'm the boss, you're the employee."

"What could I tell you? If I had said anything — about the merger, about the fraud — think of the extra pressure it would've put on you. I'm not saying you would have betrayed a confidence, but it would've been stressful for you. Or that's what I believed."

Ellen recalled Abrams' phrase — "pillow talk". She decided not to repeat it to Don. Abrams had already repented, and Don would be very angry if he knew exactly what Abrams had said to her. And she was leaving anyway.

"All right," she said at last with a smile. "I accept that your superior experience was right this once — but just this once!" Then she frowned. "I know you explained to me that what

Abrams told you persuaded you that you didn't have to regard me as someone to be protected — but what did Annabel say?"

He smiled, and said softly, "Ever since I realised you really intended to leave, it made me imagine what life would be like without you altogether, and subsequently I've been impossible. Annabel was the one person who could winkle out of me what was wrong — and she told me in no uncertain terms what a fool I'd been, and how I'd better hurry up or I might lose you completely."

"I think I might like your sister very much," Ellen said. She was beginning at last to believe that what was happening was not a dream, and that she wasn't going to wake up suddenly to find that Don didn't really love her. But did he? He'd told her he was attracted to her, that he wanted her to understand why he had behaved as he did — but wasn't he making one enormous assumption about her and her feelings for him?

Between them on the table lay the remains of their sushi. The fish were gliding peacefully in their pool, and the music on. But suddenly, instead of feeling deliriously happy, she was feeling angry. "You think it's as simple as that, do you?" she heard herself saying. "All this time you've been dictating to your emotions, and now simply because you've changed your mind, you think I'll fall into your lap like a — like a prize plum. When all the time I thought you — and you never trusted me enough even once to tell me. Even whatever it is that's been troubling you — about feeling restless."

"I acted from the best of intentions — can you forgive me? I was trying to think for both of us. I'm sorry I've ended up hurting you. And I know how you've thought for me too — you warned me that the gossip might be more hurtful to me if the newspapers should get hold of it. But I don't expect you to fall into my lap — anyway, would you have even listened to a marriage proposal then? You were so interested in your career, and proving yourself, wouldn't I have come out a very poor second?"

"Maybe — but you could at least've tried," Ellen stated contrarily. "I don't know — I must get away — I must think." And she tossed her napkin down, stood up and blundered her way out of the restaurant, losing her way in the paper screens and stumbling past other people's tables. It wasn't till she reached the pavement that she realised she'd forgotten her shoes. She had just successfully flagged down a taxi when Don appeared, carrying her shoes, and told the taxi driver to drive on.

"There you go again," she said. "High handed as ever — that's the first time I got a taxi straight away."

For answer he turned her round and pulled her into his arms. "I can see I'm just going to have to get tough with you. What more does a feller have to do to make himself plain? I love you, I want to marry you — but it's got to be a partnership. If I promise I've changed, that I'll let you in on all my secrets from

253

now on, you've got to promise to let me give you a helping hand from time to time, OK? And I'll let you in on one secret right away — I'm restless because I want to sell up and move out of the Big City, and I really didn't want to tell you that. I know how you love it."

"Oh, Don," she sighed, leaning against his chest and knowing that this was where she belonged. "I promise. I've been crazy about you all the time — I nearly told you I loved you once before, on the veranda that night. Then you let me go and I was devastated. And as for moving out, when were we ever so close than beside the sea?"

He began to kiss her forehead, her cheeks, her nose, while murmuring, "I've never felt like this before. We were destined for one another, and everyone knew, but we wouldn't accept it. Do you accept it now?"

She returned his kisses. "I accept — I love you and I want to marry you." He held her tighter, his mouth touched hers, then he drew back. "Just one further confession — that weekend by the sea? I knew you were going to be there, and I simply couldn't keep away. I told myself I only had your best interests at heart!"

"More confessions? Don — cut the talk and kiss me. And that's an order."

"Yes ma'am!"

Their lips met and, arms firmly holding each other, the jostling, teeming crowds of New York City had to open up and move around them. Don and Ellen, now that they had found each other, were not to be moved.

THE END

NURSE CAMDEN'S CAVALIER
Louise Ellis

Nurse Camilla Camden hadn't yet met the new Senior Surgical Registrar but she thought he sounded a perfect horror. However she forgot all about him when she went to the hospital Fancy Dress Ball, and there met the Cavalier . . .

THE BELLS OF HEAVEN
Nan Herbert

Alex is sure she will never be happy again when her parents are killed. But she eventually returns to the hospital as a staff nurse. There she meets Elizabeth who becomes both her friend and her enemy . . .

DR. BRENT'S BROKEN JOURNEY
Jane Lester

An ordinary train journey, and yet it changed Dr. Brent's life, for he was brought back to the hospital with unexplained injuries and amnesia.

NURSE LORNA'S LOVE SONG
Kathleen Treves

When Lorna was jilted, she poured out her heartbreak in a love song — and it helped her to meet a man who could at last take Douglas's place.

THE BUTTERFLY
AND
THE BARON
Margaret Way

When cattle baron Nick Garbutt told Renee Dalton that she was frightened to feel she knew he was right, but what did it matter when Nick already had Sharon Russell?

THE LATE AWAKENING
Nan Herbert

Nurse Fiona Robertson is disconcerted to find Richard Corder a newly appointed member of the Group Medical Practice.

THE PHYSICIANS
Elizabeth Harrison

Nurse Anne Heseltine realised that the two men in her life were becoming serious rivals — in work, and in love . . .

WITH ALL MY HEART
Christine Lawson

Austen Thurlow, desperate for a housekeeper, tells Charlotte to bring her nephews with her. But soon after her arrival, Charlotte meets unexpected difficulties . . .

NURSE RONA
CAME TO ROTHMERE
Louise Ellis

Heather had always loved David Martin — but how could she compete with the glamorous Elizabeth Chayle who was going to marry him?

ROMANCE AT REDWAYS
Jane Lester

Kenward Marr, the new RSO at Redways, could have told her that people don't always want to be "fixed", but Darbie had to learn everything the hard way.

NURSE DOYLE IN DANGER
Jill Murray

Heartache threatens Nurse Thelma Doyle when the ex-girlfriend of RSO Gavin Yeomans returns to the hospital as a very sick patient.

NURSE FOR THE SEASON
Pauline Ash

St. Chad's Hospital always took on extra nursing staff during the summer. But this year the intake was decidedly below par, thought Garth Ladbury. With one exception, Nurse Sally Anderson.

THIEF OF MY HEART
Mary Raymond

Olivia was just the girl Nicholas Sherburne wanted to look after his nephew while the child's parents were away. The arrangement suited everybody — except Nicholas's sister-in-law . . .

THE WILD MAN
Margaret Rome

Curupira — the wild man! No wonder, thought Rebel, the primitive natives of the Amazon used that name for Luiz Manchete. But Rebel soon realised that his only love was the Amazon . . .

FLAMINGO PARK
Margaret Way

So Nick Langford had known Kendall for years and was older and more experienced — but did that give him the right to try and run her life for her?

NEW DOCTOR AT NORTHMOOR
Anne Durham

The Kinglake family did not like Dr. Mark Bayfield but he was the only one who was likely to diagnose young Gwenny Kinglake's problem.

THE ENEMY WITHIN
Nan Herbert

Marian undertakes to care for her young niece, but her fiancé, Hugh, protests, since Marian will have less time for him. When she receives an offensive anonymous letter, Marian suspects that Hugh may have written it!

DREAM OF THEIR HEARTS
Honor Vincent

Nicky finds to her cost it isn't always possible to choose where you fall in love.

REBEL IN LOVE
Lilian Peake

Lex Moran decided that the local school should be closed down. But Katrine felt that the school should be saved, and she was determined to oppose Lex in every possible way.

NIGHT NURSE AT NASSINGHAM'S
Quenna Tilbury

Christine Thorby was expected to become engaged to Dr. Peter Temscott but the engagement never took place. It looked as though the same thing would happen when Martin Redway, the Surgical Registrar, fell in love with Christine . . .

SURETY FOR A STRANGER
Mary Raymond

Lewis Bellamore, a struggling young actor infiltrates the Shrewsbury family and he takes something from each of them . . .

DR. SIMON'S SECRET
Kathleen Treves

Deborah Markham met Langdale Simon and fell in love, little knowing that he was the R.M.O. at the hospital where she would be working.

LOVE FROM LINDA
Kay Winchester

Nurse Linda Brooke has no premonition of the impact on her life when three casualties arrive at the hospital late one night.

NURSE KATIE OF PRESSWOOD
Jill Murray

Nurse Katie Holland is thrilled to hear that the owner of a historic house, is planning to let some of it. She and the hospital almoner are delighted to make Presswood their new home.

WITH SOMEBODY ELSE
Theresa Charles

Rosamond sets off for Cornwall with Hugo to meet his family, blissfully unaware of the shocks in store for her.

A SUMMER FOR STRANGERS
Claire Hamilton

Because she had lost her job, her flat and she had no money, Tabitha agreed to pose as Adam's future wife although she believed the scheme to be deceitful and cruel.

VILLA OF SINGING WATER
Angela Petron

The disquieting incidents that occurred at the Vatican and the Colosseum did not trouble Jan at first, but then they became increasingly unpleasant and alarming.

DOCTOR NAPIER'S NURSE
Pauline Ash

When cousins Midge and Derry are entered as probationer nurses on the same day but at different hospitals they agree to exchange identities.

A GIRL LIKE JULIE
Louise Ellis

Caroline absolutely adored Hugh Barrington, but then Julie Crane came into their lives. Julie was the kind of girl who attracts men without even trying.

COUNTRY DOCTOR
Paula Lindsay

When Evan Richmond bought a practice in a remote country village he did not realise that a casual encounter would lead to the loss of his heart.